The English Lover

THE ENGLISH LOVER

Jonathan Smith

HUTCHINSON OF LONDON

Hutchinson & Co (Publishers) Ltd
3 Fitzroy Square, London W1

London Melbourne Sydney Auckland
Wellington Johannesburg and agencies
throughout the world

First published 1977
© Jonathan Smith 1977

Set in Monotype Garamond

Printed in Great Britain by
The Anchor Press Ltd and bound by
Wm Brendon & Son Ltd
both of Tiptree, Essex

ISBN 0 09 129410 X

Acknowledgements

I am grateful to Faber & Faber Ltd. for permission to reproduce 'Twice Shy' by Seamus Heaney from *Desk of a Naturalist*, and to Philip Larkin for permission to reproduce 'Love'.

Chapter One

After it was all over James never ceased to be slightly amused and, when he thought about it, somehow pleased that he met Tom and Helen at the same party.

The day began like any other. Well, not quite. He woke up, heavy-eyed and dead in the legs from reading Doris Lessing too late. He got out of bed and sat at his desk with his first cup of tea, looking at the small pile of books bought at the beginning of the holidays lying there untouched. One hand tapped with a pencil while the other slowly turned them over: *Patterns in Life and Literature*, *Love in English Prose*, *The Critical Experience* . . . his stomach clenched. He opened one at random, cracking its back, and read a paragraph or two: '. . . but we, the English teachers, are the intellectuals; downtrodden as we are by a controlling bureaucracy, we must fight the deadening cultural impoverishment brought about by . . .' Good God, it could almost be Alan Priestley talking; why on earth did he buy that? James leant back in his chair, sipping his tea. To think, 'to think,' said Uncle Vanya, 'I might have been a Schopenhauer, or a Dostoyevsky' – instead of a schoolmaster. James smiled.

And then, unusually early, the phone rang.

He dropped the intellectual in the waste-paper bin and walked through to the sitting-room.

'Hullo, James, Ian here. Sorry to wake you up so early.'

Ian Wilkins, Head of English, nice man.

'No, you're not, I've been up hours.'

Small snort.

'Look, I know I could probably have caught you at the meeting but you know what the Head's like when he gets going.'

'I do indeed.'

'Anyway, James, the point is we're giving a party tonight, last-minute job as usual, before all hell lets loose. I've asked a few people round, and Liz, of course, has given me a rocket because I should have asked you *before all others* she said.'

'Did she? Good old Liz. Thanks, I'd love to come.'

'Sometime after eight-thirty; give us a chance to get the rabble to bed; no grub, I'm afraid, lots of booze. By the way, I've asked some new people in the town, thought you'd like to meet them, and that Australian chap who's joining us for this term. Yes, Newman's his name. Well, I haven't seen him yet, but I've left a note at his address asking him and his wife to come if they can.'

'When did they arrive?'

'Don't know really, last week I think. They've been in London. I'm feeling a bit guilty about it. I wrote to Australia a month or so back saying I'd meet them at the airport, but they had it all arranged. Anyway, they just might feel a bit lost so keep an eye open, will you?'

'Yes, of course, Ian. What's his first name?'

'Tom.'

'And his wife's?'

'I don't know, I'm afraid.'

'Anyway, thanks a lot, Ian. See you tonight. Oh, before you go, how's Maggie?'

'Always talking about you.'

They laughed and rang off.

Just like Ian and Liz, the busiest people, to make the

effort. They had four children, they didn't lie in bed reading, of course they didn't. Had James thought of looking up the Australians? No, he searched the Charing Cross Road for nice first editions; and did Ian get all knotted up about creeps like Alan Priestley? No, you could bet he'd been invited too.

Time? Ten to eight. Surely he wasn't still nervous about staff meetings? No, it wasn't the meetings, nor the having-to atmosphere, nor even the paper in the pigeon-holes: it was seeing all the others again, so many of them his friends, so friendly and happy, with Cornwall suntans, a new jacket here, an extra child there, what did you do, James, eh, what did you get up to? Then, seeing his face, don't worry, James, you'll enjoy it once the first week's gone – and he would. With a second-class brain and a second-class personality schoolmastering was for you, for those who do things quite well, for nice people, and they are nice, by and large. Except for Alan Priestley. Oh, stop it.

As James ran his bath the front door snapped a letter on to the floor. He walked slowly towards it; there was no point in hurrying; it wouldn't be interesting. It would no doubt be bumph from the pools; it would not be a free copy in plain wrapper of Sexy Susan. Ah, economy label, save our trees. Wickleford postmark. James Burnett Esquire. Mother. Better bath and shave before reading it; that was only fitting.

James filtered some Pure Indulgence into his bath, making it silky. I feel I owe it to myself.

Easing himself gently into the only sensuous pleasure the day was likely to afford, lapping the water round his body, he shuddered slightly as it reached his neck. Damn, he'd forgotten his tea. Was it worth getting out? It was the same when you half-woke in the night, which was better: to lie there in warm, muzzy, niggling discomfort, or to slump along the corridor and sort it out? There would never again, at least not for another ninety-eight days not counting Sundays, be a morning on which he could soak late in the bath. The tea could wait. Tomorrow they'd all be there, moving in and out of his life: first, shiny fresh ones, then forty minutes later, surly smelly ones, comprehension yielding to the sonnet, Oscar Wilde back on the shelf, Christopher Marlowe dusted off. As usual he hadn't done a minute's preparation for the new term, and the new term was here. There had been six weeks, don't lie to yourself, two months, to think his courses through, plan them all out, and he hadn't even picked up his pen. It was unprofessional of him, and weak.

The door squeaked and snapped. That would be *The Times* for – he knew only too well – 9 September. James nudged the sponge away from the tap, turned the hot on with lazy left-foot skill, and with his right circulated the water back to Pure Indulgence. He could just see his razor. Uncle David. Perhaps he'd better read the letter now. He stretched up and felt into the pocket of his dressing gown, and opened the damp, steamy envelope.

My dear James,

This will be a very quick letter to wish you a happy term before I go into town to the shops. I expect you will have been terribly busy getting everything ready but please don't overdo it. You do have a tendency (I think it may be a family failing!) to go at things in a rather unrelenting way, and in July you looked worn out. I'm sure it's a good thing you are not producing any plays this term. You don't mind my saying that, do you?

Please let me know if there is anything you need for your flat. I enjoy browsing round antique shops looking for a bargain, beating them down by a pound or so.

You'll be pleased to hear the cottage in Wales is coming on very well. As I won't be able to get down there very often, if at all, I hope you will take every opportunity of enjoying some peace in those lovely surroundings. Uncle David is very keen you should really enjoy yourself there and feels Wales will be the spur you need. Do write to him sometime, won't you, it gives him such pleasure. I rang up Mr Price last night and he says the cottage will be perfectly livable (spelling?) next month. It's very exciting, isn't it?

Well, dear, Terence is barking away so I must go. We know how hectic your life is but do pop down for some weekends if it isn't too difficult, and please feel free to bring Sara whenever you wish.

> Fondest love,
> Mother.

Much as expected.

James folded away the letter and pulled the plug with his foot. He would give her a ring tonight; the stoic tone required it. Then, while his bath disgorged itself, James rubbed himself dry. He straightened to face a misty reflection in the mirror. He picked up his razor, wiped a wheel in the mirror, which improved things very little, and peered even closer. Although he could barely see himself he was driving a familiar road; he shoved, pulled and pushed his face. By the time he'd finished the mirror was clear: brown hair, a bit long, blue-grey eyes, a bit saggy and tired, the quick glance told him nothing had changed. Well, it wouldn't have. Why did that take so long to accept? Get a move on.

Running back into his bedroom he pulled on his trousers and socks, then forced his feet into his shoes. Where were the damned contact lenses – over there, on top of the new Philip Larkin. He put them in and chose a mildly exciting tie. *English masters hav long hair red ties and weeds like wordsworth throw them into exstatsies*. That will be enough, Molesworth. Dabbing on some after-shave, for whom he wasn't quite sure, James laid Doris

Lessing on the bedside table and pulled up the blankets. The place could do with some fresh air. He opened the window and looked out on a perfect summer morning and down on the commuters. Yes, there they were, half-running in a steady stream along the avenue, down past the bollards and into the High Street. Yes, good, good, off you all go then, very good, the justice of it pleases me. Unclench.

Chapter Two

As James walked down the avenue the rush hour of his busy, unremarkable town was abating. Mothers were walking their children to school. A woman shouted at her child who ran across James's path; she smiled I'm sorry but what does one do. Some little boys, off in bright blazers to their prep schools, touched their caps to respected passers-by. Others, wearing what they liked, scurried on. James wasn't sure which he preferred. On both sides lorries were parked on double yellow lines, unloading fruit and vegetables, and at the crossroads the big girl with thick knees stood, as always, stroking her little dog. John Denison, Head of Science, cycled by, lifting his hand in greeting and wobbled a little. Quite tall, an unevenly striding figure, James dodged across between the Volvos and Peugeots, over the tarmac clearing and into the College gates.

Why didn't he come down yesterday or the day before and work himself back in, collect the books he needed, get the feel of the place again? He looked at his watch, three minutes to nine, the Head would be on his hurried scurry from the study to the Common Room, James wouldn't find a seat at the back and he'd have to sit in the front and concentrate on looking as if he was listening. Masters always filled up rooms from the back. Like boys.

The room was loud and matey. James grabbed the pile of paper in his pigeon-hole and looked quickly round.

There was one seat left by the fireplace, next to Brian, and he pushed rudely for it, mumbling apologies. He sat down. Brian Withers, James's favourite bachelor, was doing the crossword. Perhaps he'd been there all holiday. Grey tufts came out of his ears, grubby glasses fell on the end of his nose. Through the check shirt peeped his navel.

'Hullo, Brian, how's things?'

'Bloody awful.'

'Haven't had a good time?'

'No.'

'Oh, I'm sorry. What happened?'

'Nothing.'

Brian, a Classics man, had not yet looked up.

'It's not funny,' Brian went on. 'Arse trouble.'

'Oh dear. Any particular kind?

'One doesn't ask.'

He filled in another answer, then said:

'And Aunt Ethel died. Left me a measly two thousand. I spent that on her. I got nine in the original, then the cats and dogs took over. I should have pushed her off Beachy Head that day. Nobody would have known.'

'I would.'

'You wouldn't talk.'

'I might.'

'You'd shut up for a thousand quid.'

There was a general rustling and good-morning: the Head was at his place. Everyone who could stood up; Brian compromised by half-lifting himself, doing up the top part of his flies and slumping back.

'Good-morning, gentlemen. Sit down please. I hope you all had a good holiday. I had an absolutely marvellous one.'

Mumbled oh-goods.

'Lucky bugger,' from Brian.

Short, bald and rosy-faced, the Head sat down a little

way. Most headmasters are tall, pale and distinguished, so the Head had to be outstanding to get the College, and he was; with him even the most manic headmaster-haters ran a bit thin on material.

'What's he got that you haven't got, Brian?' James whispered. 'I just can't see it.'

Brian smiled.

'Are you going to Ian's tonight?' James whispered on.

'Yes, now shut up and let me get on with my work.'

'Gentlemen, first of all I want to say how sorry I am I missed the final meeting of last term, but you may be glad to hear the manners of the school are improving. The Sixth Form Council sent me a very courteous card. Let me read it you. "At this morning's meeting the Council decided to send you a Get Well Soon message. The voting was fifty-three to forty-nine."'

A little too much laughter but not a bad start.

'But our results are, I'm sure, of more interest than my health. Colin, is there anything special you want to say about them?'

'Only a few things, Headmaster . . .'

'Quite,' the Head said.

Colin Rutherford, Senior Master, then made his usual kind, rambling assessment, fair to all, even to the unworthy. As everything seemed in good hands James switched off and looked through his pile of paper, each piece a different size: drama committee dates, room numbers, chapel plan, invitation to good sherry from the Governors, games programme, and a request for the key to Room 17. 'No', he scribbled irritably and then, like a condemned man knowing his fate, James turned over his timetable. Thirty periods, with plenty of large sets. Another grind.

James tuned back in.

'And so, Headmaster, the overall pass-rate is seventy-nine per cent, two per cent up on last year's seventy-seven per cent, and while I think we can say one or two chaps did rather worse than we expected, one or two did rather better.'

'Quite,' said the Head, meaning shut up, and Colin did.

Alan Priestley slipped a piece of paper to the Head. James peered at Alan. He looked as earnest and handsome as ever. The Head smiled and nodded at Alan.

'Perspicacious old bird. Four-three,' Brian muttered.

'What?'

'Easy. Hawk-eye. One left.'

'Gentle-*men*,' the Head's voice rose in mock self-reproach, 'I'm terribly sorry. Here we are talking about results and I find I haven't welcomed our new member of staff. As you know, Peter Collins is on sabbatical this term and I'm ashamed to say I haven't yet mentioned Mr Newman. I don't know what he'll think of us. Mr Newman is joining us at the College for one term. He's from Melbourne and will be teaching a full timetable in the English Department and is keen on games and drama. I'm sure you'd all like me to welcome him on your behalf.'

Hear-hear, rath-er, where is he, ah, over there.

James joined the eyes of the meeting, searching for the Australian. He was in a corduroy jacket, smiling thanks back at the Head. He had a strong face and curly brown hair. Around thirty, James thought.

'Why isn't he suntanned?' he asked Brian.

'Geography. Winter over there, you twit.'

'He looks nice, doesn't he?'

'I can't see from this seat, too low down.'

'Do you think Alan's nobbled him already?'

'Doubt it. Australians are very much their own men.'

'Are they?'

The Head was addressing them again – holiday courses and problem boys – when Philip Roxburgh nudged James.

'Is is true you aren't producing a play this term?'

'Yes, I'm having a rest. Four was enough, thanks.'

Philip always wrote the music for James and would miss their creative sessions. He looked a bit dejected.

'You should do something.'

'I might fit in a one-acter, we'll see.'

'Have you been away?' Philip asked.

'A bit – a week or so in Ireland, some cricket, a couple of weeks at home, not much really. Read a lot of nice books.'

Two or three masters were giving short accounts of the courses they'd been on, all very impressive. Philip looked at James and grinned.

Don't ask me.

'Any luck with the girls?' he asked, ankle deep.

Don't ask me.

'No, I'm afraid not.'

Don't ask me.

'Nothing came of Sara then?' Philip, up to his eyes.

'No.'

Cut. James took the Larkin poems out his pocket and started to read. The words blurred. It should be a rule not to ask that kind of question, not of anyone, unless an intimate conversation was established and even then James preferred not. He'd lark and joke about Aunt Ethel and arses, and in the pub he might be garrulous, indeed the life and soul of the party if he was in the mood, but he would not discuss his successes and failures with girls. There was too much common talk, lies most of it, about girls, feelings and love. Lies. Lie with her, lie on her, lie about her.

Sara. He could see her now, pale and eager, the way

she wanted to know what he was thinking. But tell me what you're reading, James, I want to know. I don't want to be left out.

Oh, let it go.

'Any bad workers?' the Head asked.

'Robbins, Headmaster.'

Baxter, Derrington, Vaughan, Hopkins, Patterson.

'Yes, by gum, I had a tussle with him last term. He was, may I say, popping off for a drink, clear as day, so I fixed him with my beady eye' – the old boy was taking himself off more and more this last year – 'and told him he was on report card. Any others, apart from the usual rogues? No? Right. Buildings and changes in the plant. Is the Bursar here? Ah, there you are, Bursar. Perhaps you'd like to say something about the new Reading Room and all-weather pitch.'

Switch off and pull out the plug. It looked as if the cottage would be ready for half term, a mere forty-nine days away. By week seven things were beginning to slide, everyone needed a break. If he left on the Wednesday afternoon he'd get five clear days there, walking across the Epynt, drinking, reading. Last year Sara would have gone with him. Who now?

'And in Faller's House the new lavatories are ready.'

'Oh, good!'

I'll ring you tonight, mother, before I go to Ian's. Would you, darling? Of course, I will.

Lush and prolific, the cricket field lay before him, the part of the College he most loved. Beyond the trees he could see rugger posts up for the new season. All wrong. James often sat out here, as now, even in winter because the place took the tension away; now he was upset by Philip's question, predictable though it was, and irritated by Alan's reminder to the Head, right though Alan was to point out the omission. It was silly to be so nettled by kindness and thoughtfulness. It was immature. At twenty-seven he should be able to deflect friendly probing, every bachelor this morning – except Brian – had probably been asked similar questions. People wanted to know if you had a girl and if you didn't it was best to pretend you slept around. People were like that; it was normal. Didn't parents and voters like their doctors, schoolmasters, vicars and prime ministers to be married? And if you were married and had girls, well it was naughty but normal. A little indulgence.

Anyway it would never have worked out with Sara. Some parts were all right, and there had been good moments – but there was no point.

The prepared firmness of the cricket ground satisfied him. Even at the end of the season, rutted and scored by boots, it looked perfect. James bent down to press the surface: a professional touch, caught from TV, in his case pointless because he didn't know what he was pressing for. Perhaps the Australian played. James heard a shout. A group of colleagues standing on the edge of the field beckoned him over for coffee. He put a conscious movement into his walk and joined them.

Chapter Three

For some silly reason, even when he knew he'd be with close friends, James always felt ill-at-ease before a party. His manner became perfunctory, he padded around his flat, changed his tie, browsed through his records, then lay on the floor trying to work out the personal entries in *The Times*. 'You. I slept so very well. If it was you please tell me in the office. X.' Outrageous really, but at least he or she had narrowed it down to those at work.

He put his head on a cushion. He loved this room, the patterns in the carpet on which he played marbles as a child, which he'd taken to Oxford, been sick on, carried up staircases, made love on – if that was the phrase for it. And Julian's paintings, and his mother's. Perhaps she'd have dedicated herself to it if Father hadn't died so early and if Uncle David had been all right. Or perhaps not at all. There would have been more children.

James was lucky to rent this flat and would be hard-pressed to keep it if his mother didn't help out. Thirty-one steps up, the flat ran along the top of a solid, broad red-brick Victorian house. His mother called it 'little more than a glory hole', James preferred garret, while his pupils awarded it penthouse. James rolled over and turned up the slow movement; it cleansed his mind. At least the ghastly first day was over. At the end of this movement he'd go; he didn't want to be cheered up by the scherzo, leave that to later. That's what parties were for.

'James darling, come in, how lovely to see you.' Liz kissed him on the cheek, holding him with the merest firm pressure as his eyes slid away. Her face was healthy and open, fresh from the beaches and cliffs of Cornwall. She would have been up at six-thirty, doing the washing, before running upstairs to throw the children out of bed; then after pushing them off to school she'd grab a moment to read the paper or mark some Open University work. James did not normally like sensible women, like clubb-able men they made him unforthcoming. The very word sensible suggested brogues, exercising the labrador and bouncing on the trampoline a month before the baby was due. Was their sex no-nonsense too? But Liz he liked.

James could hear a few voices behind her, too few.

'Am I unfashionably early? Sorry.'

'Of course you're not, and anyway I need some help.'

Good. He could walk round with a couple of bottles giving him the freedom of a host to move in, out or linger. Liz and Ian would make sure those he ignored did not suffer. Far from drawing his severe lines they smiled at his intense compartments and didn't have any time for all that.

'Come into the kitchen.'

As Liz led the way James looked, as he always did, at the firm outline of her back and her light brown shoulders. Healthy, loving, balanced.

A score of double-litre bottles stood between trays of vol-au-vents and sausage rolls.

'I thought you weren't doing anything to eat. No, don't tell me, they're only mouthfuls.'

Liz laughed with good-humoured acceptance. 'Shut up, and take these in.'

James peeped through the crack of the door. There were two circles, four or five in each. Apart from Ian and Brian he couldn't recognize the others. Leaving the bottles on the hall table James ran upstairs to find Maggie. When last he read to her she nearly twisted her toes off in excitement.

He picked his way through the pterodactyls and leggo. The title on her door announced 'Maggie's room'. He knocked formally, all part of the ritual.

'You can go in,' said a voice behind him, 'but I'm not there.'

'Hullo, Maggie, how are you?'

'All right I s'pose. Have you come up to tell us to keep quiet?'

'Of course not; I want to read to you.'

'Really, Uncle James? Oooo.'

She did a hand-stand.

'No, James will do, honestly.'

'Mummy says Uncle James is right.'

'Oh well.'

The black hair bounced past, there was a high kick and somersault on to the bed. She wanted to be a gymnast.

'God, I mean, careful.'

'It's all right, they're broken. Have you seen my flea?'

'No. I don't think so. No, I'm sure I'd remember.'

'I'll show you.'

'Oh good.'

She swung off the bed and ran to the chest. Red paint was flaking off its side. She creaked open the top drawer and picked out a small perspex box, a stylus container.

'He's in there.'

'Is he?'

'I caught him in my hand and put him in a match box.'

'That wasn't easy, I bet. How did he get into this one, then?'

'Oh, he was dead. Daniel poured some petrol into the match box. I expect he went dizzy and fell over.'

'Pity.'

'Yes, and I've also got a wood-louse. It's just had some babies, they're over here.'

'Uh-huh, mm, look, Maggie, I haven't got long to read you this story, I should be downstairs helping Mummy, so what's it to be?'

'That one,' she said, jabbing her finger into the *Quangle Wangle's Hat*.

'But I read that one last time.'

'I want it again. Please.' She pulled up her nightdress and crossed her legs, all ears.

'All right. Here we go. Are you ready?' Of course I am nod.

> 'On top of the Crumpetty Tree
> The Quangle Wangle sat
> But his face you could not see
> On account of his Beaver Hat.'

After a few minutes she put her hand in James's and lay down, making him move a little closer. Before he had finished she was asleep, just like that, her energy at rest. Young girls smelt lovely. Her skin was perfect; she had a back like Liz. He propped up the kangaroo next to her elbow, bent over and kissed her. For a moment or two he looked through her bookshelves, then tip-toed out. A quick good-night to the other three? Yes, he should.

The sitting-room was now loud and hot, humming with pre-term chat; thirty or forty people were pressing and shouting at each other. James felt overdressed in his jacket. As he slipped round the door he could hear the Bigot's cackle and Philip Roxburgh's wheezy laugh. Liz waved at James and came across with her arm up to guard her drink.

'James, here you are. Come and meet Tom Newman; he's over here from Australia.'

She led James into the centre of things, holding him with her competent hand.

'Tom, this is James Burnett, he teaches English, a great friend of ours.'

'Hullo, James, good to see you,' Tom said with his hand out. He had a blue short-sleeved shirt on and strong arms. They were much the same height but Tom was the heavier build.

'How do you do,' James said and shook his hand. He had obviously been an athlete, although now a little over-weight.

'Is your wife here?' James shouted into the noise, glancing round the room.

'No, she didn't come.' Tom sipped his wine and ran his hand over his mouth.

'Oh, I'm sorry, is anything wrong, or is she just tired?'

'Na, I mean she didn't come to England; she's stayed in Melbourne. She's pregnant, you see.' Tom drank some more.

'Oh, I see.' James saw a less noisy place by the window. 'Let's escape over there.' He pushed the big window up. 'God, it's hot. That's better. When did you arrive?'

'Couple of weeks ago. I've been running all over the place. West End, Foyle's, Chichester, Stratford, packing it in like a loony. I'm gradually getting to grips with the place.'

'Great.' James lifted the bottle, Tom nodded and James filled his glass to the brim, and over.

'Oops and over,' Tom laughed, flicking his hand and licking off the wine.

'Oh God, sorry, damn silly of me, what an idiot.' James looked round in embarrassed desperation. There wasn't much on the floor. 'Shall I get a cloth?'

'Na, leave it. Yes, I've enjoyed the plays a lot, seen a Shaw, Molière, *Troilus* at Stratford – and Stoppard. Terrific stuff.'

James saw Brian with all his weight on the piano.

'Yes, I agree. Look, come and meet Brian, you'll like him.'

'Yeah, sure; could we meet up and talk about English soon? I've got a great-looking timetable but I'll need your advice on texts, where to hit the little bastards, their reactions and all that. Ian suggested I ask you. He said you're the expert.'

'I don't know about that but of course I'd love to help if I can. But let's go and meet Brian, the fat one over there, you can't miss him. He's one of the best things about this place, if you know what I mean.'

Of course he does, don't patronize.

'After you,' Tom said, putting his hand gently in James's back. They nudged their way through elbows and past enquiring hullo eyes.

'Brian, this is Tom Newman from Melbourne. He's here for the term.'

'I know that. I was at the meeting too. How do you do. Why have you come to this crummy country?'

Tom smiled defensively, unsure of the tone. 'Hell, I've wanted to come for years. I've done seven years at my school and they've given me the term off, full pay, and I'm going to screw the last dollar out of the bastards, every last cent. I intend to enjoy myself; you may not believe it but I've always loved the idea of England, everything about the place, and the English, so don't tell me all that's wrong with it.'

'Not yet,' James said.

'We're not all nasty poms then?' Brian asked.

'No more than we're bloody foul-mouthed Australians,' Tom said, shaking his head and drinking.

'Are you married?'

'Yeah, but I was just telling James, Jen's back in Melbourne. She's having a baby in April. Great timing, eh? She's feeling pretty crook and couldn't make it. Are you married, Brian, or still looking?'

'What I'm looking for is the permissive society,' Brian said.

Leave them to talk. James pushed through, taking his jacket off as he went. He was getting close to Marjorie Webster and could hear her declaiming to Alan Priestley. Marjorie was formidable and she knew she was and James liked her; an amazing woman, attired in beads, who spoke as if she was writing reviews. Bill Webster was listening, as always, and she knew James could hear.

'Bill, do you know what that Australian's Christian name is?'

'No.'

'Let's call him George and stick to it. George is a very nice name, it suits such a relaxed and powerful man. Ah, James, what is he called?'

'Tom.'

'Everything under control for tomorrow?' Alan asked.

'Oh, absolutely,' James said, moving on.

'Come back soon, James, I want to ask you something, something lit-er-ary.'

'Up your street,' Alan added.

Up yours.

'All right,' James said. He left his jacket on a peg in the hall, then went to the bathroom to wash his face in cold water. His eyes itched. He looked out of the window, down on the expanse of lawn. It was nearly dark: a large check ball lay in the flower bed and further away, in the oblong light from the windows, a doll's pram was pitched on its side. Sweet dreams, little Maggie. James drank some water. How different life must be if you launched from here each day, how minor a spotty boy's moods would seem, it wouldn't matter if a sixth former criticized your mark on his crappy essay. That was the trouble. As a bachelor you had too much time and gave it all to boys, mere phantoms touched by passing affection, while some part of you shrivelled each year until, if you weren't careful, you were unmanned. James saw clearly these signs in others and sensed the beginnings in himself: he became too intense in argument, taking a severely aesthetic view, or he might vulgarize a serious talk with tatty remarks, or pretend to be more anti-clerical than he was or, worst, become phonily philanthropic. Were these the first self-indulgent tricks, the little shams of the civilized, unsatisfied man who had boiled dry?

Don't start on yourself just yet, term hasn't started. The Australian was someone, though; not tuned in yet but with all the wavelengths, flexible but with none of the careful English politic mentality. He didn't have the odour of liberal sanctity, he looked as if he could hurt and be hurt.

James collected another full bottle from the kitchen, and, turning back into the room he caught Robert Warner's hellishly suntanned come-on-over grin. To give himself time to see who was with Robert, James raised a questioning eyebrow, pretending he hadn't quite grasped what the grin meant. It was all right: Sue, his friendly wife, a teacher at the local comprehensive, was talking to another girl. James went over. With justifiable confidence Sue was showing most of her breasts.

'Hullo, James,' she said, 'I've been watching you talking to that Australian; you two are the most gorgeous men in the room. Aren't you going to give me a kiss?'

'Hullo, Sue, how are you?'

'Fine thanks.'

And your breasts are.

'James,' Robert said, 'this is Helen. Helen Craven. James Burnett. Helen's just started teaching at Sue's place.'

'Oh, really? How do you do, Helen.'

James half pushed out a hand, Helen lifted her eyes from her glass and motioned towards James's hand. Brown eyes. Their hands stopped a little short of each other. They laughed at the muddle.

'Damn silly business, isn't it, all this do-we-or-don't-we shake hands,' James said. 'The frogs all do, don't they, right round the café in their feeble exhausted way, the Americans are just bowled over to see every single one of us, the Eskimos do something with their noses, I understand, while we muck it all up between hail-fellow-well-met and cut-you-dead.'

Pause. And hit a low point.

'Oh well, I've said that now.' Sue led them all with her good mixer laugh and Helen smiled up at James. Shining brown eyes.

'Helen's come from London. She took the job here before she knew what the school was like.'

'No, that's not true,' Helen said, 'I like it. The kids are a bit rough but I like them. Some of them write very well.'

Don't say kids, please. Alan does.

'Helen teaches English,' Sue said.

'And likes cricket,' Robert approved.

Helen looked shy, on the spot. 'Well, I don't understand it very well but I enjoy it.'

Her fingers ran round the top and bottom of her glass. 'It's very good fun, and you can read and things, and when they all shout and no one says anything and it all goes on again it makes me laugh.'

'You must come and watch the town, then,' James

said. 'Robert plays for them and I do a bit. But I'm afraid the season's nearly over. And you teach English?'

'Yes, at all levels, but mostly the younger ones, a bit of sixth form work.' She ran her long fingers through her hair, a bit worried. 'I'm still trying to plan my courses, I haven't had much experience – I only had a part-time job last year, I couldn't get a permanent one in London.'

Then she dropped her hand down. Three or four coloured bangles slipped from her elbow to her wrist. James slowly filled up her glass, determined not to spill any on her hands, looking: soft green her dress, soft her face, light brown eyes, brown hair.

'And you teach English,' Helen said.

'Don't tell me the tie gave it away?'

'Sorry, I don't understand.'

'Oh, it's nothing, just a silly thought. Yes, that's right, I do teach English; all the time I'm afraid. No, I'm not afraid, I'm glad. But what's it like teaching boys *and* girls?'

James felt a push in the back. Ian ushered Alan into the group. Alan was pleased to meet Helen, at the local school was she, splendid, yes he'd heard encouraging reports from lots of people, turning into a most impressive place, interesting courses, all kinds of lively kids, oh quite you mustn't expect miracles but a real challenge wasn't it?

'I'd better go round with this bottle, excuse me,' James said, backing away a pace or two.

'Oh, don't let me drive you off,' Alan protested.

James filled up his own glass and watched them talk: Alan and the middle classes who pretended to be near the bread-line. You look well enough on it, Alan, aren't you on the same salary scale as the rest of us? You tell the boys you can't afford to buy meat and how you feel you were at the Spanish Civil War it means so much to you, and you let your car rust for fear of being seen washing it on a Sunday morning, your sincerely shabby clothes, your angst and your words like society and commitment – the boys think the world of you.

Helen and Alan were laughing now. James really would have it out with Alan. It was time to clear the air.

Why don't you go and teach with Helen at the comprehensive, Alan?

Here Alan would look anxious, perplexed, pained, like a late-night reporter on TV.

Yes, that does worry me, it worries me a lot.

As long as you're worried I'm sure you'll be all right with the kids, Alan, but I asked you why don't you go to teach at the comprehensive? And before you reply don't tell me you're trying to change our nasty old system from within.

Here Alan would go and get another drink, join another circle, not come back.

And, anyway, James knew he would never say it. It would be embarrassing to have an ugly scene. Despicable though it was, he preferred to seethe.

> I was angry with my friend:
> I told my wrath, my wrath did end.
> I was angry with my foe:
> I told it not, my wrath did grow.

But even if Blake wouldn't tell Alan the Australian looked the sort who would. . . . Where was Tom? James looked round, then back at Alan and Helen. Alan was leaning over, giving her the evils of TV and materialism, no doubt; she nodded and said something, he was ever so attentive, catching her every word as it fell. She pushed the hair back from her face. Get off her, you creep.

James forced himself on to another group. He half

listened to this person or that, he nodded, smiled and looked at his watch. Time passed.

Where *was* the Australian? Over there, still with Brian. Just before he could get there Brian started making look-out-behind-you faces. Marjorie Webster caught James by the sleeve.

'James, James, my man of taste, can you help me? I've been talking to Ian about a cummings poem. It's *not* that funny one about Uncle Sol and the chickens, which is the only one Ian knows of course, nor is it that filthy one about cars, but it begins

> death (having lost) put on his universe
> and yawned.

Do *you* know how it goes on? You're my last hope.'

Marjorie clutched her beads in suspense. James didn't have a clue. He looked decently thoughtful, on the very tip of the answer, but the only cummings he could think of began:

> may I feel said he
> (i'll squeal said she
> just once said he
> it's fun said she)

'No, I'm afraid I don't, Marjorie. Perhaps,' he could sense Tom at his elbow, 'perhaps Tom Newman does. Marjorie, this is Tom Newman.'

'Ah, yes, the antipodal gentleman, how do you do. Now, Mr Newman, God in his heaven alone knows why I'm on this silly poem, it could be the claret, but do you by any chance know what comes after this:

> death (having lost) put on his universe
> and yawned?'

'No,' Tom said, 'but you said the lines beautifully. Both times.'

Marjorie stared hard at him, undecided. Then she decided, gathered her beads and retreated.

'I enjoyed that,' Brian said, creaking the piano, 'but I must be going.'

'So must I, Tom. See you tomorrow morning. We'll talk about English then, all right? Where are you living, by the way?'

'Other end of town, past the station. Wall Lane.'

'OK. Good-night then.'

'Yeah, night, Brian, night, James.'

James picked up an empty bottle and keeping his eyes down to avoid Paul and Janet Hogan, he moved as quickly across the room as he could, knowing Liz was watching him go. It was a bit early to leave but he must ring mother.

How did Helen know I taught English? Did she ask who's that man over there, the one who looks . . . no, no, of course not. Robert would have said, 'Now then, Helen, let me point out a few of the people you don't know – that grey-haired guy on the piano is Brian Withers, he teaches Classics, the bloke he's with is an Australian who's here till Christmas, and that's James Burnett, he plays some cricket too, teaches English, and in the next group that's Alan Priestley, our History man . . .'

It would have happened as naturally as that.

'Going to the loo,' Brian said, 'see you at the bottom of the stairs.'

'I'll put this bottle back in the kitchen.'

James felt released. He bent down to run his hands under the cold tap in the sink; around him he noticed the lino was buckled and cracked with heavy use.

'Hullo again.' The girl, Helen, came in carrying two large empty plates. 'I'm just clearing these out of the way for Liz; there's no room to breathe in there.'

She looked a little taller out of the crowded room and, even in the harsh strip light, very beautiful. Her eyes were excited with wine. She exhaled, gosh, and half-sat on the table edge as if it was time for a quick break.

'Yes, I was just bringing in an empty bottle, too.' James pointed absurdly at the bottle, as if he'd been caught out.

'Is it late?' Helen asked, going to the window, looking out, breathing in the cooler air.

'Not really, but I've got to go soon. I haven't done a minute's work for tomorrow.'

'I don't believe it,' she turned, half mocking, half respectful. She had an unusual look altogether, with a touch of melancholy.

'It's true, I'm afraid,' which it was, but he sounded mock-humble.

Suddenly the door swung wide, making James step forward towards it as if he was moving before it opened.

'Here we are,' Liz said. 'Give me a hand with this tray, James. Lovely, thanks. How do you think it's going?'

'It's a super party,' Helen said, 'really lovely.'

Liz grabbed another tray, her face red with effort, and went out.

'James, James are you coming?' Brian called up.

'Yes, coming. Well, bye Helen. Hope to see you again.'

'Yes, I must go back in. Good-bye.'

Brian was sitting on the bottom step. He growled with pain as he unfolded upwards.

'Sorry, Brian, but I think I'll stay around for a bit.'

'All right. Come round for a drink sometime, if you'd like to.'

'Thanks, I'd love to.'

'Well, I must give the arse a bath,' he said and walked off into the night.

James hovered in the drive. He wanted to be out of the

party, but didn't fancy bed just yet; perhaps the garden was the place. He turned past the green-house, down to the far end, looking for the seat where he often talked to Maggie. Its white form came out clear under the tree. The leaves smelt good, spicy, and a twig scratched his face as he sat down. He shivered; it was getting a bit nippy, the end of summer.

Through the branches he could see the house, huge and black, with squares of yellow light, like a child's drawing. Loud laughter came across the garden, it sounded like the Hogans. They'd be kissing everyone by now, all the so near and so far stuff. More laughter. Definitely the Hogans. He was glad to have missed them. Paul and Janet, London rich. Janet tried to look the same age as her daughters, striving for the vogue mid-twenties' look, high-lighting her hair in an expensive ghastly way, and achieving merely the mid-forties. Yes, fair enough, she did have nice legs, wore knee-length boots and dresses slit up to the thigh, if that tickled your fancy. Only a buck nigger would sort her out, Brian said; but there weren't any around these parts. So, unmolested, on Saturday afternoons, in all seasons (diaphanous Liberty prints in summer, well-cut coats in winter), she and her daughters modelled themselves around the College grounds, swinging their firmly held bosoms, gathering in men-boys. Not that James disliked money or envied those who had it; he had a bit himself, he was fortunate enough, he knew his luck; and unlike many of his colleagues he could see why the unions used their muscle to grab it. Nevertheless when the revolution came (he loved that silly phrase), when the revolution came he hoped – while he and Brian ran off, puffing into the distance – the Hogans and Alan Priestley were lined up against the wall.

It was time to go, getting grumpy and trivial, and it had been a good party. James walked across the lawn. It was funny what she said about cricket. He peered at his watch. Eleven o'clock. Mother would be making the late-night drink for Uncle David. And he hadn't thanked Ian and Liz. Never mind, he'd better go and ring her. Then read for an hour or so before sleep. Work tomorrow. Wonder what sort of books she likes?

Chapter Four

'As a matter of fact I have these words of Keats above my bed.' James turned to the blackboard and wrote:

A man might pass a very pleasant life in this manner – let him on any certain day read a certain page of full poesy or distilled prose and let him wander with it, and muse upon it, and reflect from it, and bring home to it, and prophesy upon it, and dream upon it – until it becomes stale – but when will it do so? Never.

'And he wrote that in a letter! I don't suppose many of you get letters like that . . .'

'Every day,' Hopkins said. His cronies sniggered.

'I know that I don't. Anyway, please write that quotation into your notebooks.'

While they did so James looked around. Anderson, Brooks, Bradford, Dawson, Harvard, Hopkins (yes, him again, how did he get in? – clever, I suppose), Ireton, Jenkins, Levington-Percy, Thompson, Scott, Walters (Nigel, oh good) and Zatovski. Not a bad top set, considering. He ran his eye down the list to make sure he hadn't missed any horrors. Although now the third day of term, this was the first time James had seen his special literature group, the ones who might read English at University. Two or three were talking quietly among themselves, while Hopkins, a fraction louder, was performing for general benefit: and that's what I said to her, go on, you didn't, I bloody did, I'm telling you, phew, bloody hell, great, what did she do, she loved it, Christ did she.

James looked back at his book and opened it at week one, Christmas Term, Seamus Heaney's love poems. Wait for them to stop, freeze them quiet. Look at Jenkins, yes he's seen me. Look at Hopkins, so's he. He's stopped? Don't tell me he's reformed.

'Right, well of course you're in this special class now which I assume you've agreed to be in not only because you're "good at" literature, so to speak, but because you love English literature, want to know more, learn more. And anyway if you don't I do. I assume you're thinking of specializing in English because you're interested, and not because the Classics wouldn't have you in the first place, History was too much like hard work and the economists bored you solid. But if you think that at this level all you need do is read a few poems and novels with your feet up you're very wrong.'

Smiles of recognition.

'Good, so you're enthusiastic. Now to appreciate fully, to enjoy and be able to describe literature you need to *know* something, and not only meanings and ideas; it's more than simply exercising your perceptions and dangling your dainty antennae. We need to get down to difficult technical problems, trochees and terza rima, to literary traditions, to the various kinds of . . .'

Defeat on their faces, don't go too far.

'I'm talking too much, but one final point before we start. I'm sharing you on this special course of English love poetry with Mr Newman, initials TN on your timetables. He is here from Australia and as well as being an extremely intelligent and friendly person, though God knows why I should tell you that, he is an expert on both English and Australian literature.'

'Have you read any Australian literature?' from Nigel Walters, with a grin, testing the water.

'Not much, I suppose . . . Patrick White . . . let me think. . . . No, all right, Walters, I haven't. But if I was being taught by someone who knew about an unusual field of literature I'd be interested.'

Fair enough, Nigel nodded.

'Now the course we are giving is English love poetry in all ages. We shan't be going about it in chronological order, indeed the first poem I've chosen is a contemporary one, but we will be looking at love as it has been experienced and described by all kinds of poets in every style. Right, let's start straight away. Anderson, will you please hand out these.'

James gave him the photocopies of Heaney's 'Twice Shy'.

As Anderson went round the class James looked at them again. Brooks, haven't seen him before, rugger type, pleasant enough, Bradford yes, Dawson, Jenkins, too many rings, Hopkins, enormous knot in his tie, almost a scarf. Hopkins . . .

'Hopkins, do you mind not cutting your nails?'

Hopkins, straight from the beach, stared back and what-the-hell-do-you-intend-doing-about-it. I see, Hopkins, OK. I suppose you've been drinking six pints a night and all of a sudden you're a boy again and these sodding schoolmasters get on your wick, so try dumb insolence, the stock-in-trade deflater of twits like James Burnett. Oh well, on we go.

'Now please read it three or four times to yourselves, think about it, take notes, then we'll have it read aloud and discuss it. It's the mood I'm after in this one.'

James looked at the poem.

> Her scarf à la Bardot
> In suede flats for a walk,
> She came with me one evening
> For air and friendly talk.
> We crossed the quiet river,
> Took the embankment walk.

A good simple opening, Belfast before the troubles; he saw Heaney and his girl on their walk. James looked at the boys. Nigel Walters was absorbed, probably on such a walk with his girl. So was Scott, head in hands, concentrating. From the day he'd arrived, potty as they come – interested in buses – Nigel had been a promising, sensitive boy, a boy who knew, priceless gift, how to be friendly in private with a master without carrying the intimacy over into the classroom. In Brian's phrase, he understood the system. Nigel looked up, blushed, and nodded at the poem. Thanks. In minutes, seconds, sympathy can be established. James was always surprised and delighted by this feeling: a glance, a smile at an off-hand joke, looking down as another boy was rude, laughing away a bad decision at cricket, offering you the salt and pepper at lunch when everyone else was pigging into the chips – anything could do it, and usually the rapport survived acne, unfair treatment, even a whole year being brainwashed by the Bigot. Back to the poem, they'll be ready soon.

> A vacuum of need
> Collapsed each hunting heart
> But tremulously we held
> As hawk and prey apart,
> Preserved classic decorum
> Deployed our talk with art

That Thom Gunn poem they did in the Lower Sixth had the hawk and prey image; he wondered if they'd remember that. Yes, it was an agreeable fellow-feeling with boys, as long as you realized the ghost passed out of your life. Fellow-feeling, affection. It was such a difficult matter, a matter of being sufficiently involved, just so much involved, somewhere between cool detachment and full-blooded caring, avoiding the one which led to cynicism and a dry heart, the other to a perpetual adolescence or, worse, hands on knees in the Music School. It was a tight-rope. Considering everything, it was amazing so few fell.

Of course if one found the right girl there was no problem. Some girls sensed James's nature; Liz did, up to a point. James stood up and walked round the classroom, re-arranging books on the shelves. Helen too, briefest of moments though it was, seemed to catch some response. He turned round.

'Scott, please read the poem, will you, and all please pay special attention to the last part, the verse that begins

> So, chary and excited
> As a thrush linked on a hawk.

– all right, Scott.'

Scott read it, quite competently.

'Now presumably you know who Bardot was, or rather is?'

'We're not that young, sir.'

'And she's not that old!'

'Do you fancy older women, sir?'

That's the way it's going, is it, uh-huh. 'OK, OK, fine,' James said.

'Do you, sir?'

'What, fancy her, Brigitte Bardot, not really my type. She's a bit too much for me. But I'm sure you could handle her, Dawson. But I'm not here to talk about Brigitte's Bardot's body.'

'Who mentioned her body?'

'Look, the point I'm trying to clear up is an allusion, a dating, so to speak, that you might have missed.'

Ironic cheers.

'Come on, what's interesting about the mood of the poem? Dawson, how would you describe its tone?'

'Not sure what tone means, sir, but anyway this guy, I mean this poet, uh, meets this girl, they go out for a walk, yes that's right, and he's a bit shy, she is too, and they chat on a bit about this and that, he doesn't want to rush it, you see' – he grinned at Hopkins, knowing little sods – 'in case they wreck it all. Perhaps they don't want to risk it. And that's about it, yes, as far as I can see. Not bad I suppose.'

'Fine. That *is* about it. What about the river?'

'That's a bit corny, sir, isn't it,' Scott said, 'still waters and all that, the symbolic bit.'

'Do you think so? I rather like it. But on this kind of issue it is very much a matter of taste.'

'Yes, OK, but don't you think it's pretty thin as a poem, and as an experience?'

'Let's read it again, shall we?'

They did and became more serious and revealed more of the poem, more of themselves.

'Do you think there's any hope at the end?'

'Yes,' Nigel Walters said, 'a kind of tentative, qualified hope.'

Perhaps the poem was too 'easy' but they were responding – and so they should be if they'd chosen English. The bell came too soon. If they went on like this it could be a good course, and they could move on to more demanding, more complex poems, and doubtless Tom had an interesting, very different selection. One of them must do Blake's 'Poison Tree'; they mustn't forget that. The boys were leaving. James tidied his desk.

'Who've we got next?' Hopkins asked Scott.

'Priestley.'
'Oh, great.'

There were only a few in the Common Room, all reading, all enjoying the early days before the marking swamped everything. Legs stuck out from behind the papers. James looked on the table for *Punch*; not there; he looked round to see if anyone had it. No.

'Oh, Klepto's still at large, is he? Who's pinched *Punch*? So to speak.'

The *Telegraph* crumpled down. 'They forgot to deliver one,' Colin Rutherford said.

'Oh, sorry.'

James sat down next to the *Guardian*. 'After you with that, Ian.'

They all read. James flicked through the reviews: some bitchy, some bland, some encouraging.

'James, you must think me a bit wet for not knowing, but is it all over with Sara?'

'Yes, weeks ago.'

'Ah.'

'Yes, I'm afraid so. Oh, I don't know.'

They went on reading.

'What did you think of that girl the other night – Helen? You seemed to be getting along very well.'

Liz must have been watching. James felt himself blushing.

'Really? Did you think so, I didn't notice; she certainly seemed very nice, but she looked all taken up with Alan Priestley I thought. I hardly spoke to her.'

So silly, this defensive dissembling. Ian cared for him. Ian could be trusted. In bed and in class James had gone over every word he'd spoken to Helen, brief encounter though it was, he had later added the sound-track; he'd replayed every word she'd spoken, sifted it through, polished up a few phrases, done a literary criticism on its tone, meaning, nuance, until he was almost – but he warned himself against fantasies. But if Ian thought there was a possibility . . .

'Are you playing tomorrow?' Ian asked.

'No, I've given up for the season, and anyway I'm refereeing some dreadful match, but I might get down to see the last hour or so.'

'By the way, I mentioned the idea of playing to Tom Newman; he said he wasn't too keen, but if they're short he'd help out. Oh, here he is.'

'We're talking about you,' James called.

Tom dropped a pile of books on the table. 'They all are. Gidday, James; hi, Ian. How're you?'

'Not too bad, you?'

'Struggling, trying to find their naked spot. Do they know as much as they seem to?'

'Who?' Ian asked.

'Five E.'

'No,' James said.

Flushed, Tom sat on the table, dangling his legs, with desert boots on.

'When they smile it's really insulting, isn't it? Can you punch someone for smiling in England?'

'Well it's not normal. What do you think, Ian?'

'No, on balance, I wouldn't.'

'How about a few beers tonight?' Tom suggested, standing up and smacking his stomach.

'Yes, fine.'

'Great, beaut, where?'

'The Plough. Eight-thirty? I'll pick you up at your place if you like?'

'No, I'll find my way. What about everyone else?' Tom asked, motioning to the newspapers.

James shook his head. Not the others, thank you.

Chapter Five

Six o'clock, twenty overs to go, either side could win. James lay face down on the grass with an untouched half of bitter. Tom drank as if born to perpetuate Australian myth. With lots of coffee before school and judicious deep breathing between lessons James had nursed himself through morning school, carefully carrying his head. He did once speak sharply to a sloppy boy but was far too weak to pounce. In the open air, while refereeing in the afternoon, his brain cleared a little but his legs sagged. Finally James lost his temper when the scrum half kicked the ball in his face, making him cut his lip on the whistle.

Only three wickets left and fifty needed to win, an intriguing situation for Sassoon's prose. Robert was still in, though. To avoid bar talk, James had walked round the ground, with Sassoon on his mind, to this quiet spot under a tree. They'd talked about Sassoon in the pub; Tom wanted to know how James rated him. James said very highly, especially his prose, those descriptions of the Weald, of simplicity, of mental anguish, of cricket, of war, horses and men. No mention of love, Tom said, of girls or women or marriage. True, but there's an unspoken warmth in every sentence, a love of England, a limited kind of Englishness, maybe, amateur and withdrawn, but full of a kind of love.

'Yeah, English to the hilt,' Tom said, 'but then so was

Lawrence, so was Forster. What about *their* loves and hates, what did they think of the English?'

And so they drank and talked of books and England.

His face close to a crack in the brown outfield James closed his eyes. Through his cheek he felt a lump pressing so he rolled on to his back. The firm earth warmed his muscles. Behind his head he could hear the ball being hit, thunk, yes, no, feet pounding, stopping, get back you idiot, howwasseee. Run out at the vital stage. Typical of the town.

Well, the term was going now, and even if those fourth-formers needed some firm handling (especially Wright swinging back on his chair, shouting out the answers), he was beginning to enjoy himself. If the English boys were too statuesque for Tom perhaps he'd like the full-blooded Wright – and you can have him, mate.

James watched an over. His head thumped. From this level each blade was taller than the fielders, a Gulliver game.

'James? It is James, isn't it?'

What? Yes. He sat up, the evening sun hurting his eyes.

'Hullo, Helen, how nice to see you.' He began to scramble to his feet.

'Don't stand up, please.' She sat down next to him, quickly. He sensed her perfume.

'You're not playing, then?' she said, putting down her shoulder-bag.

'Ah well no, it's a pity but I've been involved at the College, couldn't really get away. Robert is playing, though.'

'Yes, Sue told me. Is that him out there now?'

'Yes, that's right, the one with the big green cap – it looks like an Australian cap from this distance.'

'Do they wear green ones?'

'Yes, big baggy ones and when they put them on they go mean and hungry.'

'Is the Australian playing, the one at the party?'

'No, he's not.'

'Are you winning?'

'Let's have a look. I nodded off, as you saw.' James focused his blurred eyes on the board – 'Well, we still could, one wicket left and ten to make. I doubt it. This bloke couldn't last an over.'

'Oh, don't be too hard on him, it's a difficult game, isn't it?'

Helen leant forward and put her chin on her arm. Her perfume again, or was it shampoo; she'd obviously just washed her hair. The same bangles. Her arms were brown and he noticed a long scar, with stitches on her left elbow. He liked that.

'What have you been doing since the party?' James asked.

'Painting the flat and teaching. The smell of house paint makes me feel sick. I've been dying to come down here all afternoon.'

She was watching the cricket intently as she spoke. He looked at her long skirt. A minute or two passed. The silver chain round her neck touched the grass; she seemed very relaxed with her body. 'Oh, well hit!' Suddenly the ball was bouncing over the ruts towards the boundary on James's left. A panting, heavy-limbed fielder pounded after it and gave up well inside the boundary when he saw James stand up. James fetched it back from under the trees and threw it, a little self-consciously but professionally, to the fielder waiting, surly, hands on hips.

Helen smiled up at him. 'That was a good hit by Robert.' She turned back, her shiny hair falling forward.

'Yes, only five to win.'

Unless it was so good that you couldn't tell, and that was something in itself, she had no make-up on except on her eyes. There was something amused about her expression. His face felt warm when he lay down beside her. If she knew he was looking at her she took no notice.

'How's school?' James asked.

'So-so, quite good really. I haven't had time to think yet.' He put his chin on his fore-arms too. He pulled up a few blades and chewed them. He could hear his heart beating against the ground.

'Oh *well hit*!' from the pavilion, and clapping. Helen sat up.

'It's all over, we've won,' James said, not moving.

Helen stood up.

'How exciting for Robert, he'll be so pleased, won't he?' She looked down at James with a touch of self-mockery at her girlish enthusiasm.

If he'd got up first he could have helped her up.

'Yes, he's a good player. Shall we go for a stroll round the ground?' he said. She looked at her watch; he looked at her shoulders. He got to his feet.

'Yes, let's, but I must go and change soon.'

But you look fine as you are. Why don't you spend an hour or two with me? We can go to The Plough for a quick drink; I feel like one now, my head is fine, and then back to my place, I'll play some music, we could talk. Who do you like reading, who are your favourite novelists?

'I've got to be at Ian and Liz's place for supper at eight. Liz rang up this morning and asked me. Isn't she kind?'

'I'll drive you, if that's any help; I've got my car down here.'

'Well, it would be but I came on my bike. Thanks anyway.' She walked on in a lazy loose-limbed way. They

47

passed rows of cars; fathers were folding chairs away into the boots and the children hit one more ball into the bonnet, were shouted at, and stopped.

'Where did you go to University?'

'London. I left a year or so ago. I suppose I rather messed around, couldn't get a decent job – I think I told you at the party; I lived with some friends, got fed up with that and then I saw this job down here.'

'Are you glad you came?'

'Yes, yes I am. How long have you been at the College?'

'Oh, five or six years; too long, perhaps. I think I ought to get out.'

'Do you enjoy it?'

'Oh, yes, I do. But it's not quite as simple as that, is it?'

> No. I have never found
> The place where I could say
> This is my proper ground
> Here I shall stay.

But he couldn't start quoting now!

She looked at her watch again. 'I'd like to talk but I must dash.'

'Yes, I suppose so. Did you enjoy the party the other night?'

'Very much. I met so many nice people.'

'They're not all nice.'

Helen looked hard at him, brushed by his edge. 'I know that.'

'I mean you mustn't be too impressed,' he went on recklessly.

'I'm not.'

James was waving his hands about. 'What I meant was, it's a superficial kind of thing, isn't it, all this clever talk at parties, trying to be wittier than everyone else; it's all right in its own way, but it's not what matters, it's the kind of person you are that matters, isn't it?'

'Yes, of course it is.'

'Yes, I'm sorry, of course you know that.'

Hell.

They walked on, in front of the pavilion. He could smell the bar. Too late to put it right now, let it go.

'Will you be coming down next Saturday?' James asked.

'Yes, I might. Will any of you from the College be playing?'

'I doubt it, but I might watch.'

'Oh, wait a minute, is that the twentieth? I think I've got seats for the ballet at Sadler's Wells. Do you like ballet?'

'Yes, well I've only been once, but I enjoyed it.'

He went with Sara. It was ghastly; not the ballet, which was beautiful, but afterwards they walked across London and Sara begged him to quote Wordsworth on Westminster Bridge and he couldn't; and wouldn't if he could.

'I'm sorry, I really must be going.'

'No time for a quick drink?'

'I'm afraid not, but it's a nice idea.'

She was lifting her bicycle upright and stepping on to it. She looked rather like a schoolgirl, very beautiful.

'Have a good evening, anyway; please give my love to Liz. Anyone else going?'

'Yes, I think Liz said one of the other masters at the party was going, Alan someone, I think; the one who teaches History.'

'Yes, well you'll have a great evening, I'm sure.'

'Thanks, bye.'

He walked a few paces behind her.

'We must have a drink sometime.'

'Yes, I'd like that.'

She pedalled away, then turned and waved cheerily. James faced the pavilion. He walked into the smell of damp shirts, talcum powder and feet.

Alan Priestley! God.

Chapter Six

A letter to Uncle David was overdue and now, while the sausages were cooking, seemed a good time. James had worked throughout the first ten days of term, only making it twice to the pub, so he had some spare hours for letters and phone-calls. He poured himself a large sherry. I owe it to myself, drank the top inch, filled it up and sat at his desk. He could always ring home and have a word with Uncle David but, assuming he'd bother to wheel himself across to pick it up, he tended to be curt; besides, his uncle was a civilized man who enjoyed receiving letters as he enjoyed writing them, especially well-rounded witty ones to *The Times* or serious, thoughtful ones to James. Although it meant he'd see even less of James, the cottage in Wales idea appealed to him because he believed James 'had it in him' to achieve something and Wales was just the place to try. This amused and flattered James. He put down his biro and picked up his pen, in deference to

Dear Uncle David,
   What a lovely present the Trollope was. I haven't time to read it at the moment, so I'll keep it to savour when I have a free weekend.
   Over a week has gone and things take their course. Nothing much seems to have changed except, as one poet called them, the rows of autumnal faces (I thought of claiming that but you may know the poet). The faces have a habit of saying the same

thing as last year as, I expect, do I. My A-Level set is quite fun and along with *Northanger Abbey* we've been looking at – this will please you – *Nightmare Abbey*. I was reading bits of the Peacock aloud in class and of course the attack on fashionable melancholy at first intrigued and then amused them. They are always surprised to hear their affectations described by someone in the 1820s.

Books! If you hadn't got me on to books I might have made some money and then I could

The front door bell. James finished his sherry and went into the corridor. By the smell of it the sausages were ready. There was another firm ring. Tom Newman was on the top step. Damn, he should have contacted Tom; he wouldn't have called otherwise.

'Tom, how nice to see you. Come in.'

'It smells a bad time, James. Sorry, I've put my colonial foot in it; I'll call back later.'

'Look, put your big colonial foot inside the door, and don't be silly. Only a few sausages in the oven, and' – he offered a hand for Tom's jacket – 'as you would say, the bastards can wait.'

Tom dropped his jacket on the hall floor, looking even larger under the low sloping ceilings.

'You've never been here before, have you? Bad hospitality, isn't it? Would you like a sherry, or I've got some beer?'

'You don't have any in the fridge?'

'I'm afraid not, sorry.'

'Sherry would be great, thanks.'

Tom sat down, a little puffed by the stairs, looking round at the pictures, the books and furniture. He nodded.

'Beaut place.'

'Thanks, I like it. Would you like a bite to eat with me? Do please. I mean I realize for a man who's been brought up on steak and eggs for breakfast a few sausages don't seem much but . . .'

'Thanks. I'll do them easily.'

Clutching his large glass of sherry Tom leant back on the chaise-longue, grinning with pleasure, slapping its back. He eased his leg up.

'How're you finding your classes?'

'Ya guessed. That's one of the reasons I've called round. Well, two really, one to discuss this love poetry course, and two to blast off a bit. It's the boys. They're so damn quiet, no reaction, bored bloody stupid.' He gulped the drink. 'May be my fault, but hell I can't get them going. Should I try the full frontal?'

'Haven't you heard about our famous restraint?'

'Shit mustard, I'll go along with a bit of that, but here I am bearing my hairy chest, wringing my withers and wanting to hit them between the eyes and, Christ, I can't tell if they're alive or dead.'

James filled up his glass and nodded him on.

'Now at home I go in with my *Othello* copies, first dodge the fruit, quell the riot, beat some thug into taking on Desdemona, trick a blonde surfie into reading the pouf Roderigo and if there isn't an Abbo around I hog the thick-lips and off we go to the bedroom.'

'Yes, well you won't get much of that here. Look, sorry to stop you mid-flux but I must look at the sausages. You'd like some bread and salad, too, yes? Good. Choose a record.'

Tom stood up to follow.

'Do you think they're putting me in the cold because I'm an Aussie or is it normal treatment for new masters?'

'I don't know, probably both. Some of them still can't stand me.'

'I don't mind being hated, that's all part of it; but it's the slowly raised eyebrow that gets me.'

He punched an imaginary gut.

'Mm, it's a nasty little game we play, giving away as little as we can, now-you-see-me-now-you-don't. They're probably trying to find out if you're thick or not.'

'That's bloody arrogant.'

'Revolting, ghastly. Look, hang on while I go to the kitchen. Hit the sherry and put on some music.'

James quickly mixed up the salad; pity he didn't have any red wine, not that the sausages deserved it, but Tom was in his stride and wine would have helped. Perhaps they should slip out to the pub. Mozart, clear and crisp, came from the sitting-room. James ground the pepper, annoyed with himself for sitting around indulging spiteful thoughts, silly piques, about fireside lefties, or getting edgy because he hadn't been invited to Liz's dinner party or a newspaper was missing, when he should have been helping Tom. He knew enough about English boys to anticipate their little tricks and if he'd dropped in to Tom's classroom after lessons and asked the right casual question of one of his form he could have caught the tone, and mentioned what a good guy Mr Newman was – whereas he'd merely made one rather cool useless remark to the special lit. set who were (Hopkins apart) fairly civilized and not likely to give any trouble. Tom arrived loving the country and would have a poor view of the English if this went on, and we'd deserve it.

Holding the tray on his knee, James opened the door. Tom was crouching down looking at the bookshelves and did not hear.

'Nice stuff,' James called, nodding at the record player. 'Sorry to have been so long.'

Tom smiled and straightened.

'You don't mind me looking at your books, great collection, wish I had them.'

'Have you seen the Trollope; on the side there, my uncle sent it me, first edition. Yes, do. Lovely, isn't it?'

Then they both tucked in, munching and listening.

'How's your wife? Jen, isn't it? How is she?'

'Fine thanks, everything going all right. Sometimes I feel a bit mean about it all, but I couldn't bear to miss this place.'

'Even with the slowly raised eyebrow?'

'Hell, I'll learn to love you all in the end. *And* another drink please.'

James stood up to refill his glass.

'Do you miss her a lot? Sorry, stupid question, daft remark. End.'

When he got back James said, 'Right, now what poetry, or plays, are you planning for our group?'

'OK, I'll tell you what I've got. Some Byron; I thought "When we two parted" might be good for starters, some of those bi-sexy Shakespeare sonnets, will-he-will-she-what-was-he, and what else? They don't know much about the Elizabethan lyric, so Sidney's "My True-Love hath my heart". James, dear James, can you continue this line, "My True-Love hath my heart and . . ."'

'Don't Marjorie me,' James said. Had he only known Tom ten days?

'And to start the ball rolling if Byron fails me I've got those golden oldies Marvell's "To his Coy Mistress" and Herrick's "Gather Ye Rosebuds, girls, old time is a-flying".'

'You're quite right about them being thin on the Elizabethan lyric. You might try some Chaucer, especially the well-thumbed pages.'

'Chaucer with my accent should get them going.'

'It's a good selection, though, you'll go down well.'

'Really? Thanks.'

'But don't pinch all the good Shakespeare sonnets. I'm doing a couple of those.'

'There's plenty to go round.'

'Shall we go to the pub? It only took me three days to recover from the last session. I'm afraid I haven't anything else to offer you and I fancy a beer or two.'

'Great. Your local?'

'Yes, let's.'

They went into the hall, Tom picked his jacket off the floor, and they crashed down the stairs two at a time. The plaster shook.

Tom said, 'Any chance I saw you going into The Plough with a girl the other night?'

James jumped down a few more, trying to keep up with Tom.

'Yes, I was having a quick drink with a girl I met a couple of weeks ago.'

'Good on you. Get in there.'

Chapter Seven

If his lesson on Arthur Hugh Clough's poetry was going to be successful James would need at least an hour in the Library, checking up on parallels, confirming exactly what happened to one of his English heroes. What had broken and made Clough, broken the man, made the poet? What brought Clough, the star of Arnold's Rugby, head boy and top scholar, to lose his faith and drive, to become one of the first honest doubters, the liberal intellectual to whom so many were now drawn? When, open-mouthed, James first came across Clough's poetry in his Oxford Library he read it with disbelieving pleasure: the man said everything, he understood everything, he understood James. James bought every edition of his poetry, read every article on him (climbing to the top of endless stairs to uncover a boring article in the *Wisconsin Review*), for he felt a sense of homage. The years had qualified his admiration a little but now in the school Library, while the late September sun burned through the high windows, he enjoyed re-discovering the poems. But he could not stick to his task, his mind was elsewhere, and anyway he knew, deep down, he knew enough to teach Clough's 'Amours'. Perhaps he should mark the Lower Sixth essays on 'Kubla Khan'. They were due back tomorrow.

His eyes half-shut, itching in the light, he looked up the Coleridge poem,

> Oft in my waking dreams do I
> Live o'er again that happy hour

then out of the Library windows, down on the fading lines of the tennis court and across the roofs of the flat little houses to the fields beyond. Some good hours down there, playing tennis with Sara; what an excitable game she played, talking, yelping, pleading if her shot was drifting out. Back to the poem. Had things moved on a bit with Helen? Back to the books. Yes, just a bit. They both liked George Eliot.

James read the essay in front of him. This was splendidly penetrating criticism, every concept neatly expressed, who on earth had. . . . He looked at the name on the front. Redding. Didn't know he had it in him, he's lifted it. No, that's right, he wrote well in the exam last term; he just can't be bothered unless he's stirred and 'Kubla Khan' obviously has fired him. Re-kindled himself, James leant back in his chair and re-read the poem, the river of his imagination set free.

In every cubicle boys were working. James drew strength from the collective effort. Perhaps there was a Clough there. But could one be produced today, out of what tensions would he emerge? For a few moments James had been aware of a slight background hum, gradually becoming open chat. He pushed back his chair and went round the bookcase. Hopkins, his feet on the table, was talking to another boy. Both mouths worked on Mars bars. Why did dogs work so hard to keep their bad names?

'Look, do you mind, you're meant to be working.'

'Oh,' from Hopkins, one eyebrow raised.

'Yes, you are, please be quiet or leave the Library.'

Hopkins's side-kick sauntered off, moving his head in a silly-twit-that-he-is gesture. Hopkins took one foot off the table and chewed steadily on.

'And why are you wearing a track-suit top?'

Hopkins looked up slowly.

'What's wrong with a track-suit top?'

'Nothing, *per se*, except it's not the right dress for a library. You wear track suits for games.'

'Mr Graham doesn't let us. We have to take them off.'

Deep breath.

'I'm not interested in that. You can't wear it in the Library.'

'Petty rules, typical of this place, enough to make you sick.'

'OK, it's petty and that's the way it is and if you don't like it get out. We don't eat our peas with our knives, that's a petty convention too, and we don't pick our noses in front of the Headmaster, and that's hypocritical no doubt, but by and large I'm on the side of the peas on forks and the non-nose-pickers, and one or two of us still draw the line at combing our hair in public or eating Mars bars when someone is talking to us.'

'My friends don't mind me eating Mars bars when they're talking.'

'You, Hopkins, are a boy, I am a master; if you want to wear that track suit and eat that thing you can leave the Library, and if you don't like it that's just too bad.'

Slowly and with skilful bad grace, Hopkins took off the track-suit top.

'Thank you.'

'Don't mention it,' Hopkins said.

Leave it now, leave it; that boy bit was a mistake.

Too upset to mark, too shaky to think, James sat down in his cubicle. Half an hour left before his Clough lesson and Hopkins would be there again, fouling it up.

James collected his papers, put Coleridge back, and went to look for Tom in the Common Room. All the way to the Library door he could feel Hopkins's knife quivering between his shoulder blades. Still, he'd be seeing Helen for another drink tonight and he'd have time after the class to go home, have a bath and read some Larkin.

'You remember last week we looked at "Twice Shy", that Heaney poem, the one some of you weren't too keen on; well today I want to take you back a century, to the 1840s and 50s, to Arthur Hugh Clough.' Briskly James filled in the necessary background. 'Now, bearing in mind, for purposes of contrast, that famous Herrick poem you did with Mr Newman the other day, "Gather Ye Rosebuds", let's read the Clough to ourselves.'

Heads went down. Gradually they seemed interested, even that yahoo Hopkins. True, a couple were swinging back on their chairs, creaking the backs, but they couldn't be expected to drop all their poses; they needed theirs as James did his. Now, who was it to be? Harvard wasn't a bad reader.

'I should have said that it's an *extract* from a very long poem, "The Amours de Voyage". Perhaps you'd like to start reading, Harvard?'

The boy could not catch the conversational spontaneity; a nice boy, though, Harvard. Suddenly he stopped.

'Could someone else read, sir, if you don't mind?'

'Oh, why? I thought you were doing very well.'

'I'd rather not, sir, honestly.'

'All right. Ah, Walters please.'

And Nigel Walters read. Within three lines his intelligent sensitivity and natural understanding rendered the tentative, vulnerable atmosphere, the man on the edge of an experience he might not be able to handle.

I am in love, meantime, you think; no doubt you would
    think so.
I am in love, you say; with those letters, of course,
    you would say so,
I am in love, you declare. I think not so, yet I grant you
It is a pleasure indeed to converse with this girl.

As when an actor holds the audience a strange quiet fell on the class, but he mustn't over-praise, favourites and all that, and it might inhibit the others.

'Fine, thank you. Now, any reactions, any order, we'll tidy up the ideas at the end of the lesson.'

'What did you say his dates were, sir?'

Harvard was interested, good.

'1840s, 50s. Why?'

'It's just that it seems so modern. It doesn't read like a nineteenth-century poem at all. I mean it's almost as modern as the Heaney poem, apart from the Bardot reference.'

'Good, quite, ex-actly. Now, why, *why* – don't do your *Jumpers* bit – 'what do you expect of a nineteenth-century poem? What does mid-Victorian mean to you? I ask it in the sense that a student in a hundred years' time will ask what were the 1970s like.'

They talked about God, compulsory chapel, love poetry, and what being young now or then was like, about the establishment, the Thirty-Nine Articles (what?), standing up for what you believed in, Vietnam, Tennyson, Arnold ('a friend of Clough, yes, Matthew Arnold, not the Headmaster one'), then James leapt up and read a bit, which brought them on to Lytton Strachey; it was going well, it really was, and then back to the poem. He ought to make it up with Hopkins; this was the moment.

'Right, now what is the tone, what is the mood here, in Clough? Hopkins, what would you say?'

Hopkins looked up, embarrassed.

'Well, he's not sure, is he . . . he's feeling his way in.'
Pause.

'Quite, that's right,' James said. 'A different world, isn't it, from Herrick's "Gather Ye Rosebuds"?'

'Is it?' Hopkins added, smirking.

Chapter Eight

The Plough was half full, just right for a drink. James hated full pubs, the smoke got in his eyes, while in an empty one words hung in the heavy, stale air. Helen looked more beautiful each time. Tonight her clothes seemed French, neat and casual. She had a new, closer hair-cut. James felt words beating in his head, his hands felt tense.

'Cheers,' he said as they settled down in the corner. 'How did things go today?'

'Better, yes much better. They're becoming more responsible. I think I might take them to see the Zefferelli film – that should bring it alive for them. They've probably never seen a good Shakespearean production.'

'I saw it done in the open air once, at Oxford – in a garden, forgotten which college. All those undergraduates leaping around among the trees, and when it got dark and the moon came up and the trees rustled it was very romantic. Very. It didn't finish till midnight.'

'Not much chance of my lot going to Oxford, though,' Helen said.

'No, no, I suppose not. Can I come and look round your department sometime – I'd like to see it, find out the differences?'

'Of course you can. I'll fix it up with Tony. When the dust has settled one night I'll show you round in peace.'

She looked across the bar, smiling. 'Honestly, some of the things they say!'

She put her drink down, laughing, despite herself.

'Really?'

'Mm.'

'What sort of thing? Swearing?'

She picked up her drink, demurring. She had lovely hands, with two simple rings; none of the clusters, thank God.

'Oh, you can imagine, James, surely? Mm, this red wine is good – warming me up.'

'What do you mean, things like f this and f that?'

Helen nodded, half-amused.

'But what do you do?'

'Ignore it, what else can I do? Also they go at three-thirty, unlike yours; except for once a week when we have Extended Day, lectures and seminars for seniors and parents.'

'Isn't that the thing Alan Priestley's just joined?'

'Yes, he lectures on Modern History – on Wednesdays, the 1930s next time.'

'That'll be good. He knows his 1930s.'

'Yes, I've heard he's brilliant. A lot of the staff go and the kids seem to like him. I heard one girl say she wished he taught her.'

'Perhaps he should. Do you do anything in the evenings?'

'On Thursdays I go up to London for an Adult Educational Course, painting; I go to the Life Class.'

'You paint? I didn't know.'

'Yes, I've always painted. In fact I didn't know whether to go to Art School or University, but English won. Still, I intend going on with painting. I really love it.'

'What's it like at the Life Class? What happens, what sort of people go? Drink up, I'll get you another.'

'All sorts, really. What happens – well, it's what you'd expect. We have a nude, man or woman, it's a man this term, and I'm working on a series of studies. It's a relief on Thursdays to get away to the Poly; we're all there because we want to be.'

'Doesn't it attract all the randies?'

'Oh, James, everyone thinks that. Especially people like you. Perhaps it does – I haven't noticed they're randy.'

James bent over to her. 'Do you have a mirror I could borrow, please?'

'A what!'

'A mirror, a make-up mirror.'

'Good heavens!'

'One of my contacts has slipped.'

She rummaged in her bag, laughing. 'No, I'm afraid I haven't brought one.'

'Will you excuse me a moment?'

James went to the next table and asked, for Helen's benefit, the same question. The woman there gave her husband a we've-got-a-right-one-here look, glanced round the room to see if she was on Candid Camera, and gingerly handed her mirror to James. He corrected the lens and collected another lager and red wine from the bar. He liked this cold beer; Tom had got him on to it.

He put the wine in front of Helen.

'I hope that's warm enough, it doesn't feel it.'

'James, you are funny, honestly. Cheers . . . it's nice here.'

She moved her bag and he sat close to her. 'I didn't know you wore them.' She was still amused.

'Oh, yes, haven't you noticed I'm rather starey?'

'No, you're not.'

The fire was brightening their corner. He leant back, pleased with her, pleased with the pub, pleased with the mirror business: he hadn't produced plays for nothing. It was an ordinary pub, it wasn't rough, there were no trendies, and no clubby men; ordinary and nice, difficult words perhaps but they meant something to James.

'What are you thinking about?' Helen asked.

'These people.' The local shop-keepers, a gardener or two, an undertaker, commuters; people who wanted, without being offy, to keep themselves to themselves. Everyone was friendly and let you be. Over the years James had drunk in most of the pubs and settled for this one.

'Tom says it's what England's all about.'

'How is he?'

'On the go the whole time. Look, I know it sounds like can I see your etchings but I would like to see the kind of paintings you do, if you don't mind.'

'I'm not very pleased with them, I never am, but yes, if you'd like to. Most are in my flat and some in London. I didn't realize you were interested in art. Sometimes I think I'm only teaching for the money and that I want to paint, and then I feel something different the next day.'

'I know what you mean. But I envy you the painting. I'm purely critical. I have an uncle who thinks I might write one day, but I doubt it; Uncle David – he's always encouraged me.'

'Who's Uncle David?'

'That's a very long story. It'll take all night, some other time. But going back to this critical business, I remember when I was at University I was asked to review a critical book on the literary critics. And I overheard some people criticizing my review and I thought they were wrong. And then I thought: I'm criticizing these people criticizing my review which criticized a book which criticized the critics who criticized the creative act of someone else.

Don't you think perhaps all that's going a fraction too far?'

'Much too far.' They laughed. 'I believe in the real thing.'

In a minute he'd suggest they went up to London, when there was a free weekend, to see the Blakes at the Tate. He couldn't go this Saturday as he had promised Tom he'd watch the Masters match 'for a laugh'. But what did she mean by 'especially people like you'? Before he asked her back to the flat for a coffee he ordered another lager and red wine. He looked back through the smoke haze at her; she smiled at him, relaxed in her seat, her legs long and coltish. Her beauty came across to him.

Chapter Nine

On the way down the drive James fell into step with a group of boys, talking of this and that. As they went round the corner he could hear a girl's feet running after him calling, 'James, James, James.'

The boys turned and he turned. Liz came up, flushed; she didn't care what the boys thought. The boys walked on, with a quick scandal to warm the afternoon.

'I thought you'd never hear me. I've been chasing you for a minute.'

'Sorry, I was miles away. Are you going to the match? Is Ian playing, then?'

'Yes, isn't he an idiot at his age! You'd think he'd have grown up by now.'

'Oh, it might be fun.'

The rain began to fall again. It would be a dark, murky October afternoon.

'Is Tom playing?' Liz asked.

'Yes, he doesn't know the rules, he plays that wild Australian version, but he said he'd have a go.'

'He's fun, isn't he?'

A group of young boys in duffel coats came up behind. 'Afternoon, Mrs Wilkins; hullo, sir, off to the match?'

'Yes, wouldn't miss it for the world.'

'You haven't a chance, sir, we'll pulverize you.'

'We'll see.'

'Course we will.'

They ran off. Liz and James walked behind them, down the lane and across the river. The water was hardly moving; a heavy rain mist hung over the bank. A bird scuttled near the edge.

'I haven't seen much of you,' Liz said. 'What have you been up to?'

'Nothing much. I've been busy, I suppose. In fact I haven't even been home yet this term; haven't even written for a few weeks.'

The shouts from the ground grew louder, then there was a lull, a high-pitched cackle and a roar of laughter. Someone was making a fool of himself. They hurried on, squelching into the field.

'Maggie sends her love – she keeps on asking about you.'

'I know, I'm sorry. I must come round soon.'

'Don't be silly, I'm teasing. How are things with Helen? Sue told me you're seeing quite a bit of her.'

They could now see the players, indistinguishable in mud.

'How does Sue know that?'

'They do teach at the same school! Don't you want anyone to know?'

He didn't want to fall short, that was the point. There was another roar and clapping. James busied himself looking. The Head, Colin, Brian and a group of senior men stood behind the posts. Liz joined some wives. James went across to find out the score.

'Ah, James, here you are,' the Head said, 'a tale of woe, I'm afraid. Sixteen–four to Youth. Brian will give you the details.'

Brian looked unlikely to do this.

'Oh, dear, never mind,' James said and sauntered off to the corner flag, hoping to find an agreeable bunch of boys. If he couldn't he'd go home and ring Helen.

Anyway, Brian's account in the school magazine would be much funnier than reality.

A group wandered past him, ragged and loud. Embryo Hopkinses.

'What a tackle! Christ, who did that? No, God, I don't believe it, it was Half-Alive. Half-Alive's got some guts.'

James didn't wish to know that lot. If he was playing could he take that, could he hear himself mocked? He couldn't even handle a simple question from Liz about Helen. As if there was anything to hide. Dammit, it wasn't even as if anything had happened.

'Hullo, sir, enjoying the game?'

'Hullo, Nigel, I've only just arrived. I haven't caught up with the action. Tell me.'

'Well, it's a bit of a farce really, quite funny though. The masters are, well some of them are past it.'

'Aren't any of us playing well?'

'Mr Wilkins is still pretty good, and Mr Priestley is fast.' The scrum was getting down near the corner flag, grunting, straining, breathing like cows in a fog. The masters were defending desperately.

'How's Mr Newman playing?'

'He's got a kick like a rhinoceros, but he doesn't seem to pay much attention to the rules. He takes people off at the throat.'

'Is Miles Hopkins playing by any chance?'

Nigel giggled.

'And where is Mr Newman playing?'

'Full back. Over there.'

Tom stood, looking much trodden on, with his hands on his knees, his stomach heaving. He was concentrating totally on the game.

'Is it right that Mr Newman's definitely leaving this term?'

'Yes, I'm afraid so. He's got to go back to Australia, his wife's having a baby.'

'Really? I didn't know he was married.'

'Oh, yes.'

'It's a pity he's going, he's a great bloke. He's a very good teacher and we have lots of laughs.'

'I can imagine. What sorts of things are you doing? Look, let's walk a bit shall we, my feet are soaking.'

Nigel talked freely; his light, nervous voice described Tom: 'he turns up a bit late sometimes and he's not a great marker, you don't mind me saying that do you, because I'm not criticizing; he teaches us more in thirty minutes than most masters do in forty, and he tells stories. Yesterday he imagined a dinner party he gave in which he put D. H. Lawrence and Jane Austen next to each other. He's fun, and he makes us work.'

'I'm sure he does. Would you like to come back for some tea? I don't think you've ever been to my place, have you?'

'No, I've always wanted to, but I've got the Quartet rehearsal in quarter of an hour, so I can't really. Could I drop in some other time?'

'Of course. Let's go anyway, this one looks lost and won.'

They walked back, soaked to the skin. Nigel's long hair was stuck down on his face.

Just after six Tom rang him to go to the pub with the others, to 'lend a bit of class' to the occasion, but James hated rugger talk and wanted to write a letter. Tom pressed, he resisted, determined to be far from laughter and the mock-heroic.

Dear Uncle David,
Partly to make up for not visiting you, partly because I want to be alone, partly because I want to talk and you to listen, I

am going to write you a proper letter. For some reason (again I don't know why one feels what one feels, do you?), the whole living thing seems so difficult. You remember that passage in *The Mill on the Floss*, when Maggie says to Stephen (I know a little Maggie here, by the way, so it makes me smile to write that name) 'It seems right to me sometimes that we should follow our strongest feeling – but then such feelings continually come across the ties that all our former life has made for us – the ties that have made others dependent on us – and would cut them in two. If life were quite easy and simple . . .' (I won't go on, you can look it up!) It seems a bit pompous writing that down but you know what that book means to me and copying out such passages, or ticking them, is I suppose a way of defining one's life, of saying my life can be found here.

I cannot work out why one day life is simple, one day difficult, one day niggly, when there's so little difference between the days, and contemplating that exhausts me, trying to define the joys and sorrows of the difficult moments 'dries the sap in my veins'. (Two marks if you recognize that one.) You, thank God, will not attempt to give me easy answers. Nor will you say, 'Turn to God'. You might say, 'Think about what the Bible says, read it all, there is much good in it'. I'm glad you say that kind of thing. I don't go to chapel much. I might go tomorrow. I don't know. Writing like this might take me there.

But what I want to know is what has helped you through all that pain? Fortitude? The Roman virtues? Is every day difficult to you, I don't mean just physically (I remember you saying to me that 'Pain is painful. Forget all the claptrap about the nobility of suffering'), but philosophically, is it painful in that sense too? You must have asked all the questions of God and yourself. Would God think my kind of questions uncalled for?

He wrote on for pages and after he'd finished he worked hard all evening: for Uncle David. He broke off now and then to stretch his legs or to re-read a passage, to find a parallel, to look up a definition.

Work was a joy.

Chapter Ten

By mid-afternoon on Sunday he felt weary. Solitude shrank into loneliness. He rang Helen.

'Hullo, are you free – for a walk? We could go now for an hour or so before it gets dark, or are you busy?'

'No, I'd like to come. Where shall we meet?'

'By the stile, Mill End, in a quarter of an hour, all right?' There was a hazy, white sun, and the walk across the park, through some alley-ways and small red-roofed houses, was James's favourite. It opened out into flattish, low lands. With a long dark brown scarf wrapped round her she was waiting for him. To help her over a high gate he held her hand and kept it. There was quite a cold wind. In the next field they could hear model aeroplanes buzzing. When they got to the river James announced that the game was to see how many leaves you could catch.

'In how long?' Helen asked.

'A minute. I'll be time-keeper. Get under those big trees over there. Don't cheat.'

'How can you cheat? Don't be such a teacher! Does it matter if I drop any?'

'No, keep on grabbing more. Just be careful you don't fall in the river. Ready, steady, *go*.'

He watched her swirling round. She caught fifteen.

He gave her his watch. 'Go!' she shouted suddenly.

He started running, diving to catch, leaping up,

stuffing them in his pockets and up his sweater. He won, easily. She laughed, pushing the hair off her forehead, complaining, 'You didn't say we could use pockets.'

'IQ, obvious.'

'Right, be an aeroplane,' Helen said, her hands on her hips.

'What?'

'I said, "Be an aeroplane".'

'What now, *here*?'

'Yes.'

James stood looking at her.

'Helen, I don't too much mind cavorting around like babes in the wood, not too much, though I don't particularly fancy Hopkins and his heavy mob coming round the corner, fags in mouth, to see Twitty Burnett catching the leaves as they fall, but I won't be an aeroplane. Sorry.'

'Oh, well.'

'Sorry, definitely not.'

'Meany.'

'Yes, OK, fine, I'm a meany. But don't let me stand in your way. You take off, by all means.'

'I'll be a glider. They don't have engines.'

And she was. The wing-tips of her scarf flew out at the side and she was off; around the field she glided, hovered, turned and dipped. She must have done it before, she didn't make a sound. It was eerie.

'Don't crash,' he called, on edge.

She quietly came back to him. He wanted to take her hands, wrap her scarf round her neck and kiss her. They walked for a few paces.

'Autumn, it's going,' Helen said.

'Yes, you can see why so many poems have been written.'

'Can you remember any?'

'No, well, just lines, like "raking up leaves, raking up leaves", which isn't very demanding.'

'You're not worried some of your boys might over-hear you?'

'No,' he said, ruffled, 'I'm not.'

The sex shop in the Charing Cross Road, that was the only time he'd been worried about being seen by boys. Behind every shelf he saw the grinning leer of a fifth former; and as he looked at the most amazing inventions and wondered where they went he expected someone to say 'And a Happy Christmas to you too, sir'. When he passed the glass door he saw, the very image come to life, he had his old raincoat on. So he hurried back to Foyle's where he cleansed himself in the Romantic Poetry section. None of this free verse.

They were now walking back along the river, and through the darkening fields to the town. At the bottom of the steps to his flat he said, 'After you, you'll be exhausted by the time you get to the top.'

Helen went ahead. James looked at her legs all the way up. At the top she stood aside while he opened the door. He half fell in.

'Damn silly mat, it's time I got shot of that thing. Come on in.'

He pushed open the sitting-room door.

'I've just realized this is the first time you've been here. Excuse the mess it's in.'

'It isn't a mess.'

'No I know. Don't know why I said that. Coffee, tea or a drink?'

Was it masculine to live in a mess?

'Super views.' Helen was on tip-toe, looking out. The pavements were touched by the street light.

'You should see it in the early morning. Much better. The summer is lovely up here. Coffee?'

She turned round and took her coat off.

'Mm, please.'

'Would you like something to eat?'

'No thanks. I had an enormous lunch.'

'Do sit down, please, put on a record, read a book, etcetera, do what you like.'

He laughed, 'I'll shut up, won't be long, put the fire on.'

When he made the coffee – Sara – Sara came to mind. Sara always put on Brahms, not that you should judge people on that, it's superior, nasty, but she did; he noticed it and disliked it. True, she took an age to choose but that is what she always chose. He spooned out the coffee, feeling the withering away, the gap in his stomach, even the tone of her voice; damn, damn, he didn't want her back now, nudging her way in. Not now. He and Helen had a couple of hours ahead of them. Take in the coffee, talk, relax.

Helen was on her knees, still choosing, her back hunched over the rack.

'I'm hopeless, I never know what I want. You choose, please.'

'No, no, honestly, you.'

'Please!' She swivelled sharply and looked hard at him. He flicked through a few, stopped at Boccherini. There on that couch, on the carpet, in the bedroom he'd made love to Sara; the practical way she took off her clothes, undoing buttons and hooks without looking at them; come and kiss me she said, she didn't want to be helped; in the end it had to end, it wasn't likely to be any good, was it, and it did end, guiltily, in the Charing Cross Road.

He put on some 'cello pieces.

'You look fed up,' Helen said, sitting on the carpet. 'I'm sorry, it's just that I get flustered if I have to choose, even a book for someone's birthday. I spend hours in book shops and come out angry and depressed. Sorry.'

She lay back. 'And anyway this music is lovely.'

She held up a novel she'd picked out. 'Can I borrow this Angus Wilson?'

'Yes, do. I'm looking forward to Wales for the reading. Have I told you we've got a cottage there?'

'No, how nice.'

'You know, when I was at school I was more alive in books than in life. I actually thought I was living in Middlemarch. I wanted to be Lydgate and marry Dorothea.'

'You'd have had to kill Rosamund.'

'I was a doctor, and much as I wanted to strangle her I'd decided on a subtle poison. My Housemaster thought I was a bit odd, but as one boy in our dormitory was really nuts no one noticed me.'

'What do you mean "really nuts"; in what way?'

'Oh completely. It all started with the Ashes. Cricket? Yes, of course you know. Well, he was so impressed by the Australian cricketers, all those tall rangy men beating us up, that he obeyed the Australian climate. So, in the middle of our summer he piled all our spare blankets on his bed, because it was cold in Sydney. That's what I call nuts.'

'And in winter he had nothing on?'

'Exactly. So I was pretty normal. Reading books wasn't that odd, after all.' She picked up one of the cushions and hugged it. 'And where's this cottage in Wales, which part?'

'Hang on, I'll get a map of the area.' James went to his desk and took a few minutes searching until he found the right one.

The air in the sitting-room was now very warm. Helen had taken off her cardigan. She had a blue T-shirt on. He spread the map on the carpet. She sat up and bent over.

'Now,' James said, 'this is where the M4 ends. Then you drive about eighty miles north into those mountains and we're about here,' he put his finger on the spot, 'just on the edge of that spur, there, can you see?'

She bent closer to follow his directions. He could see the scar on her left elbow and the stitch marks.

The phone went. He stood up.

'Excuse me a moment.'

He picked up the phone.

'Hullo.'

'Is that Burnett?'

'Hullo, yes, James Burnett here, who's that please?'

'Why don't you get fucked?'

'I'm sorry. I didn't quite catch that.'

'Yes you did, Burnett, I said why don't you fuck yourself?'

Pause.

'I'm sorry, you've got the wrong number.'

He put down the phone. God. How awful, how bloody awful. His left hand started to shake. He held it with his right. James felt his face burning hot. Hell. Did he really say that? Yes, of course he did. He said it with hatred, real hatred. The voice – James didn't recognize it.

'Do you know the area well? I once went further up north, to Snowdonia on a school trip, it was when my parents were splitting up, and those ghastly mistresses – they used to make us so mad. Have you been up there?'

'Uh, no, not really, no. Well I have, a couple of times, you know.'

Surely to God no boy would, no one was that screwed up; it didn't sound like Hopkins, surely James hadn't been that nasty in class, had he? Perhaps some fool just looked up the book, jabbed at a name? It didn't sound like a boy's voice – perhaps Hopkins put someone up to it?

'Anything wrong, James?'

'No, no, fine.'

'Well, don't sit there staring at the wall. You were telling me about Wales, the cottage, I know where it is now, but that's all. Is it near a river – oh, I could look myself, couldn't I; yes it is, a small one.'

The tone was mocking, hard too; it was a voice which knew how to hurt, not just anyone, but me.

'Yes, sorry. Look, Helen, I've got to do some work – I've just remembered a couple of things I really ought . . .'

'Oh fine. Yes of course. You'd better.' She stood up. 'I'll go and start on that novel. I could do with a nice early bed and a read. You're all right, aren't you; you're sure there's nothing wrong?'

'No, no of course not. It's silly of me to forget how much I had to do before tomorrow and I was enjoying myself so much talking to you they just slipped out of my head. Let me get your coat and I'll walk you home.'

'There's no need honestly, no I mean it. I've walked home through south London often enough and you'd better get going on all that work. I like your place, by the way. And thanks for the coffee and the walk.'

'Good-night. See you soon.'

'Bye.'

He watched her head and scarf disappear down the stairs, and shut the door. He looked at his watch: nine-thirty. He felt sick. He'd only eaten a couple of sandwiches all day; he'd better eat something solid. In the kitchen he rattled around looking for the frying pan to cook some eggs but felt even worse at the thought. Oh come on, this obscene stuff goes on all the time; it's one of those things, you have to take it in your stride. He took a can of beer from the fridge and gulped. The cold shocked his stomach. Back in the sitting-room he heard a slight hum and turned off the record player. He walked round to the phone, looked at it, sank down in a chair, picked up the receiver and dialled.

'Is that Tom?'

'Yeah.'

'Tom, this is James. I'm sorry to bother you when you're probably having a quiet evening but I wondered if I could come and see you?'

'Sure, any problem, anything wrong?'

'Well actually, it's rather awful but I've just had an obscene phone-call. I'm shaking all over.'

'Jeez, the bastards. Better if I come across to your place. This isn't exactly a classy spot.'

'Are you sure? Would you?'

'Those stairs will be the death of me but for you I'll do 'em.'

'Thanks, thanks a lot.'

'Hey, James, don't hang yourself.'

'What happens if they do it again, now?'

'Get your games whistle, right? Put it by the phone and when the foul-mouthed little shit starts you blow a full-time blast, that always stops them, then next day you look for all the ones who are deaf, absent or shell-shocked.'

'You've had them yourself?'

'Yeah.'

'And you think it's definitely a boy?'

'Hell, I don't know, but I should think so. Who cares? Look, hang on, I'll be round.'

Chapter Eleven

Over the next four or five days the sickness shaded down into a nasty niggle. To cover that, and the little scratches on his brain, James threw himself into his teaching. He bounced into his special class, slamming the door in good humour.

'Good-morning, here I come to cast my phoney pearls at the feet of some real swine. Now, earlier in the term we've looked at "Twice Shy" and "The Amours de Voyage" and since then you've been reading, at least I hope you have, some of Browning and Keats's love letters, to their wives and girls I mean, not to each other, and with Mr Newman I understand you've been adding to your knowledge of Chaucer with bits of "Troilus and Criseyde", is that right, and Marvell's "To His Coy Mistress"?'

'Yes, sir.'

'Good. Well, today I want to go back to our greatest writer and look, not at his dramatic poetry this time but at one of his sonnets. And what are the themes we usually find there – you may remember from the Lower Sixth?'

'Time, isn't it,' Scott suggested, 'the passing of time?'

Don't go on too long. Make them experience it first.

'Yes, the transitory nature of our flesh, if you like – but what is timeless?'

'Art. Keats's urn and all that, poetry.'

'Yes, Dawson, well done!' Good for a second-row forward.

James smiled and went on, 'The timelessness of literature. Now, the one hundred and fifty or so sonnets have attracted lots of theories: who is the Dark Lady, who is the boy, who is A. L. Rowse, no, you know what I mean, but look, let's read it.'

After thirty seconds of silence: 'Was Shakespeare a queer, then?' . . . Hopkins.

James kept his eyes steadily on his edition of the sonnets. He waited for a few seconds.

'It depends what you mean, doesn't it? Would it please you if I said yes, or would you prefer no? I don't know whether he was or not; I don't know whether he knew whether he was or not; and he isn't here to discuss it in depth. Perhaps it would help if you thought of him as the Pouf of Avon?'

It wasn't good enough. The room was quiet. James looked up for the first time since he started speaking. Most heads were down, no one was looking at him. He'd better go on; sensibly.

'I think it is possible for someone of Shakespeare's nature, someone of his emotional and spiritual capacity, perhaps it is possible for anyone, to love a woman and to love a man, in all kinds of ways, and not to be ashamed of it – and I think it's possible to understand that without getting either medical or Swedish. I'm not sure what that makes him, and I don't care – I deny it's even a moral point. I suppose it depends what you mean by the words. On balance I'd prefer to stick to the poem and leave the rest. Would you please all go back to the poem? Thank you.'

James tried to read the poem but could not. They sat for ten minutes or so in total silence. He looked at his watch. Like Lawrence he'd sit and wait for the bell. No, he'd chosen this life and it was almost a fair question – perhaps Hopkins meant it seriously but he just couldn't put it well; he was a victim of current attitudes. He looked at Hopkins: a likely story! Still, he wasn't going to lose.

'Will you take notes, please, and don't let your mind slip over the difficult lines. Perhaps it would be better if we made this a writing period. Let's have your opinion of the poem on paper, open it up for me.'

You need many faces in defeat. His eyes cleared and focused:

> Let me not to the marriage of true minds
> Admit impediments. Love is not love
> Which alters when it alteration finds,
> Or bends with the remover to remove:
> O no

The words soothed him, the best sonnet of them all (well, arguably); but there was no chance of getting this lesson off the ground. Even this perfect poem could not clear the air.

Damn boys. James sank into one of the big Common Room chairs. Hopkins, the little bastard. If this was going to happen what was the point of sharing personal views with them, it 'all went down the same abyss'. No, the Lawrence anger would only provoke it further, and many of them are enjoying the love poetry, most of them are. They were as embarrassed as you were, embarrassed for you. Nigel looked mortified. You must balance on it, James, you have to give and you have to be hurt. But if they push me too far I can't, I can't.

Helen, he must phone her. Nearly a week since that lovely walk. It was rude the way he forced her to leave, especially after that moment of quick delight when he felt he knew – perhaps he should have told her about the call. After all, what was the point of being close if you couldn't talk, and she knew all about that kind of thing, f this f that, remember. It wouldn't be easy to talk about it to her but perhaps he should. Helen. He thought about her often, at his desk, or in the Common Room, or in bed when the day eased into night; as the boys in their beds dreamt of 'their' girls, or had nightmares about the matrons. When the cinema clock gets exactly to eight I'll put my arm round her, that's what James said to himself, fifteen years old. He did and left it there while Rome burned and he got arm ache. And so on through the years, up and down in his mind, and on their bodies. It should be possible to talk about these things, one could inch up them, glance off, avoiding guilt, avoiding the confessional, avoiding the Head's we're-just-servicing-the-car approach.

Alan Priestley and Tom came in, laughing. James picked up the *TLS* and put up the engaged sign.

'You're looking fed up, James,' Alan said. I'll swing for him, I really will. 'Tom, tell James what you had in that essay; it's a real scream, James, you'll love it.'

Tom wrinkled his nose at the Second Time. 'Well, the question was, the old fifth-form chestnut, "Is capital punishment right?" and Davies wrote, "The pubic demands we should return to hanging".'

'That's nice,' James said.

'Anyway, James, what's up?' Alan asked.

'Boys.'

Alan laughed, irritatingly. He looked so healthy and positive.

James stood up.

'What have they been up to then?'

If you try to humour me you will fail. 'Oh, nothing very much. Just buggering up my lesson.'

'Well, they're so spoilt, aren't they, these kids. Too sheltered, that's their trouble. It strikes me every time I teach them. I was talking about the French Revolution this morning and they're so smug it's sad. The only Revolution they know about is the sixties. They need a cold blast of fresh air. We do too much for them, spoon feed them, give them far too much for their own good.'

Oligarchy and Apathy by Alan Priestley.

'Do you mean they're not good honest maintained boys like you?' Tom had wandered over and sat down, reading.

'Oh don't be silly,' Alan said, 'you are touchy; for goodness' sake.'

'Yes, OK, I am touchy but I've had enough for one day and can do without you analysing The System.'

'I was only trying to help.'

'I know. Thanks.'

Alan, too good-natured to be hurt, sat down next to James.

'That's all right, I get ratty sometimes. Oh, by the way, I was talking to a friend of yours the other night who teaches at the local Comprehensive. Helen Craven. Very attractive, intelligent girl, isn't she? Lots of fun. She came to one of my lectures and we had quite a chat afterwards. I must say I do enjoy those sessions; they're a real challenge. They've asked me to give another course after Christmas.'

'Oh, really?'

'"Girl accused of ill-treating prawns."' Tom read out the headline in a loud voice. 'Trust the Poms.'

'Yes, mostly modern history, of course; the Depression, thirties, the Second World War, that kind of thing interests them. If you break it down into clear-cut compartments it works with a large audience. They ask excellent questions afterwards; they're untrained, that's the problem.'

Tonight Mr Alan Priestley will lecture on Liberalism and the Bogus Dilemma.

'Yes, well I hope it continues to be a success,' James said with a little smile. 'I know you're greatly admired there. Now if you'll excuse me I've got to do some work.'

James moved past him; then, controlled and livid, hurried to the Library. As he pushed open the swing door he told himself to cool down. Control yourself. He pulled out a chair in his favourite cubicle. Gradually the irritation lessened; his mind and body settled. He looked round the Library, how many were sixth formers, how many were young. It was important, as he kept telling the Head and Ian, that the Library was attractive for the young ones.

Although a new boy, it wasn't long before James realized that he was the only junior in his house who lived books. Then he met Weston; he was in another house. Going along the muddy clinging paths by the shadowy water, lots of trout if you knew how, he talked and talked to Weston. James learnt to skim across the river; he was thirteen. The stones whizzed, skippingly across, sometimes Weston's almost took off. They went up small hills and got their best shoes dirty. Have you read *Rogue Herries*, Weston, oh, it's pretty trashy really Weston said; he was seventeen. And they discussed *Reynard the Fox*, not bad, it does at least have narrative pressure, Weston said; what does that mean, oh, it drives you on, you see; and they wondered whether in literature you could tell lies, stretchers Mark Twain called them, did he, that's a good word, and whether the witches on the heath in the school play were frightening or funny. They arranged to meet in the Library in break the next day. Try to find out something about literature I don't know, Weston said, and it wasn't easy unless you asked silly things, but then even the biggest fool could ask more than the wisest man can answer, Weston said; well George Bernard Shaw actually.

But the walks had to stop. Mr Meredith said so. Why, sir? Because he's rather old for you. Is he, sir? Yes. How do you mean, sir, we talk about books. Anyway he is a bit old for you, you know, better to find a chap your own age. Come on now, that's not too difficult, surely.

Just impossible. James knew it now and he knew it then, but at thirteen he groaned inside and a dusty cloth fell over his feelings, and later, in his dreams, as his mind shook in its socket, he calculated ways of murdering Meredith and all those who killed affection. Or love, but it wasn't the right word, love.

He must read another thirty pages of Trollope if he was to write to Uncle David about it. He read. Then he sensed someone behind him. It was Tom, his head buried in a big dictionary. Suddenly the dictionary slammed and Tom said, 'Hey, James, let's go for a walk up the road. I want to post something off to Jen.'

'I shouldn't really, I've got all this to read.'

'Trollope? You teaching it? You're madder than I thought.'

'No, just reading it.'

'Come on anyway.'

'All right, you go on. Just let me finish this chapter. Won't be a minute.'

'His chapters are longer than that.'

'You wouldn't know. Now push off, you great philistine.' After James had made his point he got up to leave. On the way out he caught Nigel's eye. Nigel looked down, evading. Unusual. James went up to his table.

'How's things?'

'Fine.'

'Are you sure?'

'Yes, thanks.'

This isn't the place, it might be anything, his pockets may be heavy with words, crisply folded purple pages,

pages achingly read, pored over behind lavatory doors.

'Right,' Tom said, 'let's go.'

They walked up the road towards the small newsagents. On the corner the fat girl stood stroking her little dog, staring at the crossroads.

'There he is,' Tom said, pointing through the window, 'all our dreams come true. Let's go and oil his knocker.'

They went in and took their places behind two bent old ladies. Miseriguts stamped their books and blew down his pipe and dribbled flecks of spittle on their pound notes and they were grateful.

'One 10p stamp and an air sticker, thanks,' Tom said.

'We say please,' James said, 'where you say thank you.'

'It's all English,' Tom replied, placing his card on the counter, every inch of it covered with messages to Jen and their friends back in Godzone, missing ya Jen and the sun and the blood and the beer.

There was a hold up. Miseriguts was looking, unashamedly, at Tom's card.

'Only five words for 10p.'

'Sorry?'

'I said,' he dribbled a few blobs, 'only five words for ten pence. That's all you get.'

'Have you been reading my card?'

'No, but I can see it's got more than five words on it.'

'Your job, fusty luggs, is to sell me stamps. I want *one* 10p stamp,' here Tom snapped his coin firmly on the counter, 'and *one* airmail sticker.'

Two more people had joined the queue and were enjoying the scene while they pretended to choose between blue and white Basildon Bond.

'You can't put them on that card,' Miseriguts said.

'I'm not putting them on that card. I'm putting them on another card. This was a practice card.'

'Don't give me that one, I know your type. Australian, aren't you?'

Tom leant forward, his nose an inch or two from the burning end of the pipe.

'I am an Australian, and if I do swill me beer and eat me pies then so does my English friend here. And I am not a type. Nor are you. Nor are you a policeman; English policemen are nice and friendly. You are a man who sells little perforated stamps in a shop. Now the queue is building up, although it is still quiet and orderly, and I want one 10p stamp, and here is the money, and I want one airmail sticker, which, although I've only been here six weeks or so, I think I'm right in saying I don't have to pay for – yes, my friend is nodding.'

Miseriguts moved back slowly, keeping his eyes on Tom. He opened his big book and slowly huffed his way through the cardboard pages until he got to ten. He tore off one stamp. His wide flat fingers then searched in his little drawer for an airmail sticker. He handed them both to Tom. Tom stuck them carefully on his card, rolled his clenched fist over them until they were properly dry, looked up and said,

'Gidday to ya, rippa.'

They ran back to school, laughing. People in their Peugeots stared at them as they dodged through the traffic. Fifty yards from the gates they stopped.

'Oh my God, marvellous,' James said.

'Thanks.'

'Where on earth did you get "fusty luggs" from?'

'The *Dictionary of Dirty Words* – in the Library.'

'I'm impressed.'

'Aw, that's nothing, all part of the hairy-chested bit. But you're just as good at yours.'

'What?'

'Your bit.'

'What bit?'

'Hell, you know, the evasive ironic English bit.'

They were now outside the Science block. Tom stopped and turned to James.

'And, James, one thing more – in the Common Room just now, with Alan, you were wrong. Don't let it all get you down, it's not worth it; don't cut people out, take it in your stride, eh?'

'Yes, thanks. Thanks for telling me.'

'Get out to London, take Helen to dinner, you know the kind of thing.'

'You think I should?'

Tom put on his travelogue voice: 'James gave her dinner under the stars in a walled courtyard, softly lit by storm-globed candles in black wrought-iron stands.'

'Where the hell do you get all this stuff?'

'I read. And you've got over the call, yeah?'

'Oh, yes, really.'

Things were fine for the rest of the day, the boys co-operative, and the lessons soon passed.

Chapter Twelve

If he hurried now he'd catch her as she cycled home, and as there were many ways of cutting through this estate he didn't want to miss her. The little bungalows were normal, neutral and homely; on the short tarmac drives stood Ford Escorts, and along the side tiny, proud green-houses. Every square front lawn was the same size, each tended and loved. Three or four hundred yards away, across a clearing, stood the tall, grey flats, another world, the 1950s. The wind blew sharply down the straight road which led to her school, criss-crossing avenues; allot-ments, drab and bleak, opened out at the end of the estate. A few broken-down sheds were dotted around. A waste land.

James got to the school too soon. He felt foolish, standing there on the edge of the net-ball court. He looked foolish. Was he a lurker? Too young to be a father, too old to be a boyfriend; out of place and oddly dressed from the other end of town. He stamped his feet, fatu-ously. It wasn't that cold. Scurried along by the wind, sweet papers and crisp packets scraped and bounced across the yard, to land on the pile in the corner of the fence. He'd like to smell the school, get the feel of the corridors and the paint, open the cupboards, and those big windows made a place hotter, and colder. All schools felt different. He looked at the building. It was ugly. When the school came out he would observe the manners and mannerisms of the boys and girls – he liked defining things, seeing distinctions, while trying to avoid boo and hurrah words – he'd look at their styles. Would the boys swagger, hugging their mischief? How would the girls walk; was it possible to walk with style on those big shoes? How different would the staff be, would they look and dress like masters at the College, what was a master, what was a teacher? Was he a master, was Helen a teacher? Was he different from Helen – 'especially people like you,' she said, didn't she?

Within minutes everywhere was full of boys and girls, a swarming Lowry painting, but with sharper colours, the colours of new shops. Don't evade the issue, James; the colours are cheap, not just inexpensive, but cheap. Thousands, it seemed, came out. With expert flourish, cupping their matches against the wind, the boys lit up and called what're you up to tonight then hey-ey to the girls. They hurried on, follow me cheeky and find out. The boys exhaled expansively and followed, cocky, lively, the best bit of the day ahead of them. Some of the girls were very beautiful; some heavy-kneed, walked past, clump-clump, eyes on the pavement. Greens, purples, red and orange. Groups of boys, some very long-haired, some cropped, rode their bicycles with casual skill, like racing cyclists dallying – all tactics – before the break on TV. Here the tactics weren't to win but to keep Old Smelly Breath from driving home quickly to his wife. The red car blew its horn. The cyclists, at snail's pace, straggled across the road bringing him to a stand-still. They passed cigarettes to each other.

'Hey, you boys, get out of my way, get *out of* . . .'

They went on talking loudly at each other. There was a long, loud blast on the horn and an accelerating sound. They scattered and threw V signs up his exhaust, stuff you Old Smelly Breath they said. Like Hopkins, really.

'Night then, miss.'

He saw her, surrounded by six or seven girls, chatting at the tops of their voices. James backed behind the wire and circled round the net-ball court, to catch her as she came through the gap. She was protesting and laughing, her hair blowing hard across her face. She waved good-bye to them, stepped on to her bike and pedalled across the lines of the court. She looked curiously at James as she stopped, unsure.

'Hullo, what a surprise. What are you doing down here?'

'Hullo,' James said. 'It's *up* here, I always think of it as *up* here. I often walk round this part of town and I suddenly realized I was near your school. Can I have a look round? No, you wouldn't want to at the end of the day.'

'Well, I must admit I have had enough. Come back to my place for tea if you like; you look cold.'

'Yes, I'd love to. Shall I push your bike for you?'

'No, thanks, I'm fine. Is it still only Thursday?'

'I know what you mean.'

They walked on through the bungalows. Cyclists rode past in a steady stream, some turning to stare at James, casing the joint.

'Who's he then?' just loud enough.

Sniggers on the wind.

'Must be hers.'

They shouted hey-ey-ey into the wind. Helen walked her bike on, unflushed.

Little sods, James thought, they make me uncomfortable.

'Not a good day, then?' he tried.

'Oh God I don't know. I tried a Roald Dahl story, you'd think they'd like that, wouldn't you, but I seem to spend my whole time trying to get three or four to listen. Perhaps the others are coming on a bit.'

'You'll win. I bet you'll get them all in the end.'

What chance did he have here; they'd leave him – what was Tom's phrase? – for fruit on the wall. There was always total silence when James read a short story. Presumably you found out, patiently and exhaustingly, how to adjust, working your way into their world.

'Yes, the children here like you, I could see that.'

'Could you?' She looked James full in the face, her eyes tired, searching his eyes. 'Really? I hope so.'

They turned into another road.

'I'll just get a loaf of bread for some toast,' she said.

'Let me pay for it, please.'

'No, you're having tea with me.'

By the time they got to Helen's, it was dark.

'Tom doesn't live far from here, across the railway line.'

'Oh, really. I don't know this area at all yet. Come on in.'

He'd often imagined Helen's flat and he was close to it: not exactly tidy, hairdryer, sweaters on pipes, coffee cups unwashed, two chairs; not exactly comfortable, one or two unfinished paintings of the London man, Paul Klee prints unhung, letters and envelopes on the floor in piles waiting to be knelt next to, re-read and answered, a champagne cork on the mantelpiece. Ashtrays. If one lived like this one was, after all, educated. It was a kind of signature; to make love you had to throw a couple of hairbrushes off the eiderdown. Such a room was inconceivable in that row of bungalows.

'This is the first time you've been here, isn't it? Put your coat somewhere.' Helen whisked round the room, sensing his thoughts; hairdryer goes there, coffee cups won't take a minute; why Barbara doesn't do them herself I don't know, you like Paul Klee, I suppose we all do, have you read his art manifesto, marvellous, you do the toast, yes, they're my paintings, don't ask me what I'm trying to say. God, this bed is in a mess; put the gas fire on, do, it makes nice toast, yes, winter's really started.

It was excellent for toasting, almost like Oxford days, no much better, thank God all that's gone, he enjoyed this place. James buttered a piece and held it up to her hand.

'Lovely, thanks.'

He pushed the hair out of his eyes; he hadn't had it cut this term.

'I must get this lot cut.'

'Oh don't, it doesn't need it, honestly.'

She took her long boots off, warmed her feet by the fire and scrunched her toast. The room hadn't taken long; it became her. The bounce had gone out of her legs, she could feel the warmth loosening her. Thank God the day was over. She lay back against the bedspread. He knew he was being watched. He looked at his watch: five o'clock. If only she lived alone. His hands were hot now.

'What are your flatmates like?'

'Very nice. I don't see much of them, I suppose. They both work at Thompsons, the solicitors.'

'What time do they come in, then?'

'About five-thirty usually, sometimes six, it depends.'

Was it long enough, was that what she meant. It wasn't long enough, it would be awful if they came back, everything would be wrecked if they heard the door key fumbling at the wrong moment. There would be other moments, longer hours – she might come to Wales, she seemed interested. He felt her cotton shirt on his face as she moved easily into his arms, she wasn't too eager. She folded and eased under his chest. They kissed and lay back together.

'Are you,' his heart banged, 'are you doing anything much at half term? It's only ten days or so away.'

'Mm? No, not really, having a rest mainly.'

'Do you fancy a day or two in Wales, at that cottage I mentioned to you?'

'That sounds rather nice – I'm not absolutely sure but I think I can make it.'

A letter was waiting for him, it must have arrived second post.

Dear James,

How many chords your letter struck and how well you write in a tactful, searching way; that you can find time to write to me is so kind.

I can't answer your questions of course. I'm not sure there are any answers. I've read the Bible three times in my life, from cover to cover (none of this modern skimping), and I don't know the answers. The only thing I would say is that the search is always interesting, intellectually and spiritually, especially the everyday search. Like Wordsworth I believe in the importance of certain moments but I also believe in the quality of our everyday search – searching ourselves for hypocrisy, for chances to love, for chances to work.

Work! I've had some chances to love (your mother, you, people in the village) but none to work. That has, I think, been the hardest thing, by far, to bear. When you go to bed you probably feel exhausted from the emotional tension of your concentrated day, too exhausted I expect to even think of the word search. You need sleep. I know, I've seen it in your face all these years. When I go to bed I have no sense of exhaustion. You probably want to avoid crises, I plan to meet them. You get up to classes, discussion, joys, arguments, committees. I get up to – ?

So there is little chance of my giving you the answers and whether the Anglican Church will is up to you. We search in books, you and I, we find our nourishment there; and when I go I'll take books with me in my head, in my mind and deeper still. I don't care greatly for talk about culture and civilization, the words make my mouth feel wrong, but I do know the comfort of books. Give me books.

There are many things that I want to say to you one day, perhaps soon I hope, things I've been meaning to for years and which have recently clarified in my mind. Come down and we will talk.

Write to me again. Your letter gave me great joy.

Yours ever,
Uncle David.

Chapter Thirteen

Before James had settled back in his seat he was asking himself, as he knew he would, why he'd turned up. Fiercely he shut off his mind. He could do without another confessional on himself. Who was here? Across the Chapel, behind the boys, he could see Brian stuck in his pew; a little further along, among the other staff, Tom was looking from window to window. Thinking what?

James thought of the thousand and one me-in-chapel poems in the school magazine: the walls always brass-plaqued, the masters always minatory, the mandatory seas of bored faces, the shuffling feet and the smell of gowns. Occasionally a daring one mentioned a breakfast belch. What was Nigel thinking now? He was here; somewhere among the faces. James looked steadily along the rows until he saw him, head lolling on one side, face blank.

During the prayers (and expecially for Michael Roberts, our missionary in Africa) James pressed his eyes into their sockets. He tried: make me a better person, I'm so lucky to have so much, no more phone calls please, look after mother and uncle. I'm happier than I've been for some time – is it Helen? He ran his mind, jumpy and straining, over all those he loved. Then he stood up for the creed; five or six boys leant slightly closer to hear whether he was committing himself or not. After the anthem came (please make it bearable), 'In the name of the Father, the Son and the Holy' . . . . They sat down.

'A boy was showing a visiting preacher round the school and the visiting preacher said, "What sort of sermons do you chaps here like?" and the boy replied, "Not more than ten minutes and not about religion."'

It was going to be Purgatory. The very walls groaned; this was not a place to grow wise in.

'I'm afraid I can fulfil the first part but no promises on the second.'

I'll keep my mind on charity. What will Helen be doing: painting, spending the day in London or seeing old friends – or new ones?

The spruce little preacher was now telling a story about Jung, Billy Graham and St Paul – what on earth was he doing, swimming on regardless into the teeth of the Gale of Indifference; hadn't he heard of Alan Bennett's sardines? James looked at Nigel. He was looking at James. James looked away.

'Why is it we need bifocals, one vision for God, one vision for Earth?' He should be fined 5p every time he said 'why' (and Alan Priestley every time he said 'society').

'Why? (5p) Why (10p) are we embarrassed by that word "saved"? We say, "The goalie made a great save" (oh do stop trying so hard, we play rugger here), "I save with Abbey National", "Save me, the girl cried", but when it comes to God we find the word embarrassing. Why (15p)?'

James shot his hand up. *Because*, as Maggie would say, *because* it's a question of a completely different order. Isn't it? Yes, the whole school roared. Instead, they reserved for the old fruit a collective yawn; it wasn't worth getting worked up over. Ever so fractionally loudly a boy burped. A Housemaster checked who it was. Would we now have the sporty metaphor, would we soon be fighting off the pack, barging through the line-out, selling a dummy to Moloch and crashing through the Devil's tackle to score a try for God? But it ended, inside the distance, and James stood up, small inside, none the wiser, thankful only for the sound of the sentences in the Authorized version; and when Richard blessed them James prayed again, touched by the words, so plain and right. He walked out, the air heavy with a score of bad poems. Back in the vestry James waited for Tom. Tom came in whistling quietly to himself.

'And what do you think of Chapel?'

'Ian or Greg?'

'No, you idiot, this Chapel. What did you make of it?'

'Not much.'

'What did you think of the sermon?'

'I didn't listen.'

Tom hung up his gown.

'Shall we go for a walk round the grounds. It's a bit cold, but if we keep moving . . .'

'Yeah, let's.'

They nodded greetings to some boys and left Chapel behind them. The grass was deep, made thick with rain.

'You must be missing Jen? Is it miserable for you?'

'Sometimes, a lot – and I'm missing the comforts and the chance to moan – but I'm glad I came.'

'Let's have a great big moan in the pub. That always makes me happy. What are you doing at half term?'

'Scotland. I'm hiring a car, off on my own. Just the job. And you?'

'Wales.'

They walked under the dripping trees. Tom laughed, and turned to James.

'That lesson, the seven foolish virgins one, I've never been able to take that seriously – ever since I read about that Oxford don, forgotten his name, who said, "Quite honestly, would you want to be inside with those wise virgins all holding their little candles or outside, in the dark, with the foolish ones?"'

'Nice,' James said, 'I like that.'

'Look, let's go over to my classroom. I've got to pick up some books.'

They walked through the empty, clean corridors and up some steps to Room Seventeen. Tom's blackboard was covered with quotations. He sat on his desk and dangled his legs – at home – always the desert boots, even with his Sunday suit. James walked round. There was a Giles cartoon pinned to the wall.

'Would you like a curry at my place?' James said. He wanted to talk about Helen, if he could.

'Beaut. Just let me gather together a few things here – now where the hell did I put those poems, the lot they did after lunch on Friday?' He scrabbled around, cursing his desk, himself, throwing magazines and chalk into the bin.

'I like your room,' James said.

'Oh, come on.'

'No, I mean it. It's easy to relax here. I can see why the boys like it.'

Tom looked pleased and sat down in his chair. He started to talk, people, politics; he grabbed a poem off the desk and read out bits.

'Bloody good, eh?'

James wandered and listened. In the cartoon the master was saying good-bye to a skull-and-crossbones thug: 'On behalf of all your teachers, Ronald, I cannot express too deeply our sorrow that end of term brings us to the parting of the ways.' Out of the master's bald head came a thought-bubble in which he was cheerfully beheading Ronald's glum block.

'Yes, who did you say it was?'

'Robert Tillotson.'

'Yes, he's got something, he might make it one day.'

'Hell,' Tom said, 'I'm beginning to like the way you people talk. If I don't get back to Jen I'll be a gonner. Back to Jen, back to her mother, back to bridge!'

James picked up books off the shelves, putting them back in their right places.

'You don't mind me doing this, do you?'

'No, go ahead. You know I'm feeling rather guilty about enjoying it all so much. It's that Jen . . . no I don't want to go into all that.'

'Do, please, I'd like to know.'

'We met at University. You know, can I carry your books for you, see you after lectures, all that terrible American film stuff, tennis parties, beach parties, surfing, not quite blond heroes but too close. And I was good at exams. I wanted to read, or I didn't know what I wanted, but it all looked good, it felt good, *we* looked good. Dick Diver material. You must have had that feeling?'

'I'm not sure.'

'Jen's a difficult girl to grasp, I wish you could meet her, then you'd understand; or perhaps you wouldn't, you're English. I met her too early. Not that I wish to pick the bones out of that lot.'

James didn't particularly want to go any further into Jenny.

'Would you like to come down to my home for a week-end sometime? I'd like you to meet my mother and uncle. Oh, I don't know; it's a bit claustrophobic, things can get pretty tense with my mother.'

'I know the problem only too well . . . mothers!'

'You'll be a father after you get back – does *that* feel strange?'

Tom laughed. There was a feeling in the room James did not want to recognize.

'Hell. I've almost forgiven her.'

'For what?'

'For fixing it.'

James tidied the shelves. 'Oh, I see,' not sure that he did.

'Yeah, I'm a bit slow, it took me a week or so – it wasn't oops at all, no bloody oops about it. She didn't want to come to England, so she fixed it.'

'Perhaps the idea of England frightened her?'

'Why? Hell, we'd been talking about it for years, planning it, and when this temporary job came up near London she was really pleased, it had all the makings of three or four great months, then hullo, oops. . . . OK perhaps she was frightened, perhaps I should have stayed, perhaps I was leaving the family too late; anyway, what the hell.'

'Mm. Let's have a curry, pick up some beer at the off-licence.'

Tom's eyes sought out James at the back of the room, he slapped his thigh and jumped up out of his chair.

Clanking the beer, they walked up to the flat.

'I'll flex my muscles in the kitchen while you sit on your arse,' James said. 'That is how you talk down there, isn't it?'

'Just get on with it,' Tom said.

And he did.

'And here it is,' James said later.

Tom pretended not to hear. He Was Reading.

'*Anna Karenina*,' Tom said, looking up, turning the novel over.

'Haven't you read it yet?'

'Re-reading,' Tom said.

Tom helped himself to a beer and slapped his stomach, 'I'm just a glutton with brains.'

'Just a glutton.'

Chapter Fourteen

'We don't like it and neither do you', the big head on the poster said.

See you on platform three, James said, he did say platform three didn't he, for the 1.27 and don't be late and dammit it was twenty-five past and the train was already spilling over with shoppers and football supporters. James hated being kept waiting almost as much as he feared being late. His stomach ticked, clenched, ticked. He chewed his ticket. If his mother was ever out late at night, when he was a boy, he'd lie in bed staring, cold and still: she'd crashed, if he didn't move she'd be safe, no, she was dead, he'd be alone, Uncle David couldn't cope. And when the lights of the car moved fast round his bedroom walls, the agony loosened and he cried himself to sleep.

'I won't be late, I'm looking forward to it,' she said. She liked Blake.

'I'm looking forward to it, too – 1.27 OK?'

How often he'd tried to control it, like that woman in the Roald Dahl story, the one who left her husband rotting in the lift because she knew he liked keeping her waiting, but he couldn't. Perhaps Helen wasn't coming; she'd found something better to do with Alan Priestley.

Then he saw her, running down the broad steps, waving. Look out, mind that trolley. She nearly tripped but gathered her long skirt and ran along the platform.

She panted in front of him, plonking her big leather bag on the ground.

'Wow, sorry. I thought I'd had it. The phone rang just before I left, someone asking me to do something, it was a bit difficult and I started talking . . . phew . . . sorry.'

'Let's get on.'

She bumped ahead of him into the corridor. Suitcases and baby buggies blocked one way. She turned up the train. The carriages and corridors were full with red and white Arsenal scarves and big boots; young lads opened cans of Tartan Bitter, talking loudly about what they'd do to Everton, just for starters, no offence lady. Struggling and grunting they ostentatiously pressed their bodies against the window to let Helen pass. Carriage by carriage, James and Helen walked the whole train, knowing it was useless, knowing it served a purpose: Helen composed herself, James became responsive. Walking behind her was good, the heather skirt, the muted colours, her long boots showed now and then, soft crinkly brown. He liked looking at her when she couldn't see. She dressed with not too much effort, not too little, the casual skilful way. Even mother would approve!

'No good, blast, oh well, never mind,' he said, 'let's stand here.'

They stood swaying between two carriages, as the train accelerated over the last bits of open country and through the first tunnel into the outskirts of London. Helen had an attractive way of standing, he'd often noticed that, very relaxed and unselfconscious. Some girls, the Hogans for example, were so unruffled and lacquered at sixteen he wanted to ruffle them, to ruffle them very badly indeed.

In the flickering quarter light of the tunnel her skin

cooled down to pale. She wiped a bit of grit from her face. James leant across to put up the window the final bit. It slowly slipped down. He pushed it up again. She laughed as it did the same. He crouched down a little and kissed her, long and close. She drew back a little.

'Sorry I was late,' she whispered, her hands on his chest. 'I know it annoys you.'

'Oh, forget it, that was nothing, forget it. Let's have a quick drink before we get there.'

'Lovely.'

The buffet bar was crammed. James had to wait behind two men, hands in hip pockets, their shirts and jeans bulging with weight and muscle. Their young faces were hardened by outdoor work and heavy drinking; their stomachs showed over their thick belts. One nudged the other with his elbow, motioning over the carriage.

'Which one?'

'The classy bit with the knockers?'

'Christ, yeah.'

James followed their eyes and looked quickly back.

'Up and over, eh?'

'Yeah, quiet like, but when you get in there, eh? Eh?'

'Yeah.'

James went back to Helen.

'Oh, it's hopeless here. Let's wait. Sorry about that.'

The intimacy of London was good. James felt it everywhere: as they ate some sandwiches, when they stopped for coffee, even dodging through the crowds and up the steps to the gallery. They were linked together. Helen pointed out the quality of the paint, the use of symbols, the placing of shapes. James was surprised by their smallness and the strange light. She ran her hands in lines and curves in front of the pictures, you see, looking back to see if he was nodding. He looked at her hands and legs, every part seemed right – her height, the tone of her walk, the overall effect. He must tell her soon, tell her what it felt like to be him, with her. It wouldn't be easy. When he was seventeen he told that Swiss girl he met on holiday and then told his friends; and what a laughing stock he became. While the Swiss girl danced with some Italian his friends asked him what exactly he said to put her off so quickly. He'd said it to Sara, he'd whispered it to her on the floor in the flood of love-making – no it wasn't love-making, it was having sex – he'd whispered it to her in the darkness and as he said it the feelings slipped off the words. They did not want to be there and they were right. He'd mean it when he said it to Helen. He would say it straight to her eyes. 'You're so inhibited,' she said before she started gliding. No, she didn't say that, you thought she meant it. Did she? Was he? He certainly knew what he didn't want. He was put off by open emotion, that was very English no doubt, and it was a dark tunnel he kissed her in, and Tom's baby, he didn't want to hear the truth, not that it was very shocking, and Tom needed to say it. And once, at Robert and Sue's, he'd been put off by her birthday card on the mantelpiece: 'Cuddles, I love you so much, roll on tonight, Starfish', that sort of thing anyway. Awful. Helen saw James smiling and smiled back. They moved into the next room. More Blakes. On Valentine's Day in the Common Room Brian and James always had a session with *The Times*, laughing at all those messages from the chubby hubbies. The country, Brian said, is over-run with rabbits and bears. Was it a defence mechanism, as Alan would say? Would Brian really like to be Snookums to his matron's Twiddle-puss? Difficult to know. And then there were the literary ones. Hey, Brian, listen to this one: 'Sheil; Shall I compare thee to a summer's day, thou art more lovely and more temperate. Brucey-baby.' Educated Australians obviously.

'This year,' Brian said, fighting his way to his feet, 'we are so impressed by the entries we are giving three prizes and I call upon my colleague, Mr Burnett, to announce the names and hand over the cheques.'

'I will start, as is the custom, in reverse order. Third prize goes to "Bog Frog, how about a tiny bit, Mouse"; second to "Looby Loo, though we cannot make our sun stand still, yet we will make him run, Banana", and first "To Grotty, we do it, Road Runner".'

They were going upstairs to other parts of the collection. James took Helen's hand, 'Super, aren't they?'

'Come on,' Helen said, and hurried up the steps.

In a sense James preferred Julian's paintings – he knew Julian, he saw his kind, intelligent face behind the picture. On the way up they passed 'Today's Lecture: The development of English Landscape painting in the late seventeenth century. Professor A. T. Rosley, 4 p.m. South Wing. Room XI'.

'Shall we go, or have you had enough?' Helen asked.

'I don't mind really. What do you think?'

'Let's leave it, shall we?'

They went out into the noise.

'Helen, how often does Alan lecture at your school?'

'I've told you that, once a week. They're very interesting, I always enjoy them.'

'Yes, he said he had a nice chat with you afterwards, last week, wasn't it?'

'Yes, we went out to the new French restaurant afterwards. Have you been?'

Did he, did he indeed? A subtle slippery knave, a finder out of occasions.

'No. That must have been nice. Was the food good?'

'Yes, lovely, too expensive, though, I don't like having so much money spent on food. Somehow I think it's wrong. It must be my upbringing.'

Peanuts for a man on the breadline. Helen was looking at James, a small heat in her eyes.

'Why don't you like Alan?'

'I don't really know.'

'Yes you do, tell me. I don't agree with all he says, but then I don't with most people. What do you think about him? I think his heart's in the right place.'

His hands began to shake.

'And where is that? All right, all right, I'll tell you. I don't like his . . . his subtle adjustments of attitudes and vocabulary; I don't like his *luxurious* attitudinizing, and the clever way he presses the right liberal social buttons, and I'm not struck with his winning little assertions about the class system – *and* I don't like the way he smiles inscrutably when he's questioned on his own special position; I don't mind him all that much, I suppose – he just makes me sick.' He shouldn't have started, he was falling every minute.

'Good. You've said it.' She didn't look at him. They walked on down a furtive side street where the shops were grubby and stained yellow, lit only by neon chemists. The small gap between words, James thought, so small and so clear, one almost needed to be bilingual. What the hell was he getting so worked up about, so possessive; he hated the very idea of possessing. Helen had obviously enjoyed Alan's lecture, which was obviously a good lecture, and enjoyed the meal which was (although expensive) obviously good, and certainly better than the cheese and chutney sandwich James bought her.

'Look, I know it's not yet six but let's go and find something to eat. Some spaghetti and wine – I feel like being warmed up, don't you? It's cold, isn't it?'

'Oh let's walk around a bit first shall we? I love the streets, they remind me of all sorts of things.'

'All right, fine. Right, I know. Let's walk to Buckingham Palace; let's make the grand gesture.'

'The Mall. Lovely.'

They started running, across the traffic lights and under the arch, out into the Mall. He liked the way she ran. The trees, the wide spaces, the taxis, how wide, clean and beautiful it was. They slowed to a walk.

'I met a boy from your school the other day,' Helen said, 'a very nice boy. He said you taught him; his girlfriend introduced me.'

'Oh, who was that?'

'Nigel Walters, he's called. I've often seen him around the school buildings; he's going out with a girl called Jacqueline Hall, one of my sixth year.'

'Nigel. Really, how interesting!'

'Why?'

'Well, the other day I thought he looked a bit dreamy and anxious in the Library. I expect he's in love.'

Helen giggled, 'Or bored with his work.'

'Yes, I suppose so.'

A man passed them whistling between his teeth. James took her hand, suggesting, 'Let's go across Green Park. Do you know a good Italian place? Cheap, of course!'

'Yes, plenty,' Helen said, 'but I want to go to other places first.'

For half an hour she walked him across London, in and out, up and down, holding his hand firmly. Where was she going; and why? (5p)

She stopped at a restaurant, and went in first. Candles, check tablecloths, four or five choices on the blackboard.

'Perfect,' he said, gripping her arm, 'just the place.'

'I thought you'd like it.'

The waiter took their coats and smiled shrewdly as James immediately glugged two large glasses from the carafe.

'Cheers,' James said, 'and thanks for a nice day.'

'Thank you. I've really enjoyed it. And the walk.' She smiled reminiscently, 'London again.'

'I prefer the hills,' he said. 'I hope you enjoy Wales.'

'I'm sure I shall.'

'You certainly know your Blakes – you can teach!'

'That boy says *you're* the best teacher he's got, so there.' He drank some more. All those modern poems, echoes of poems, teased in and out of his mind; poems about girls on top of buses, girls in restaurants, about girls like Helen, with her nut-colour hair and her rose flush coming and going.

'I saw your friend Tom the other night, on the train down from London; he looked very depressed. Is he?'

'Tom? No, I don't think so.'

Tom, alone on the train, with no twinkle in his eye; Tom stretched across the dirty British Rail seat, staring out into the cold, wet night, without his wife. Perhaps James should have taken him to Wales, it would have been kind. No, Tom went his own way.

The waiter put down their food.

'And more wine?' James asked.

Helen, winding some spaghetti on her fork, nodded. He called for another carafe and the waiter again gave them his enjoy-yourselves smile. She looked at him, and he felt his hands and chest tighten.

When he got halfway up the steps he could hear the phone ringing. He pounded up, couldn't find his key, found it, forced the door open. There was a letter on the floor, but he ran into the dark of the sitting-room, and grabbed the phone.

'Hullo,' he said, sitting down heavily.

'James?'

It had to come.

'Yes, mother, how . . . are . . . you?'

'Are you all right, James, you sound exhausted.'

'I've just run up the steps, that's all. It's late for you to ring, isn't it?'

'James, I've been getting worried about you. You haven't been to see us.'

'I'm fine, mother, fine. I wrote to Uncle David.'

'I know you did, dear, and thank you for that. And I'm delighted you want to go to the cottage, even though it means we won't be seeing you over half-term. *Can't* you come down for a weekend, you usually manage to? Uncle David would love to see you, not that he'd ever say so.'

'I will after half term, I promise; I'm sorry.'

'I've rung four or five times today; you're never in, dear.'

'I've been up to London to see an exhibition, and then I had to dash back to do some work at school this evening, and . . . oh, you know, mother.'

Don't force me into a corner.

'I mean if it would help do bring Sara down. If you feel we don't want the both of you, you're quite wrong, my dear.'

If she didn't lay off, he'd say something he . . .

'When I get to the village, mother, do I just go to the next farm and get the key from Mrs Price? She'll be in, presumably?'

'Yes, she always in, like I am. I'm so glad you're keen on the idea of the cottage, even though it is quite a way. Now take plenty of warm clothes and a sleeping bag. There's a bed there already, but no linen. The builder says it's all perfectly ready – light a fire and warm the place. What will you do for food?'

'I'll find a pub or hotel, it's not the Outer Hebrides. I'm only going for a couple of nights.'

'You won't be lonely if you call in at Mrs Price's and ask what's going on nearby. I do wish I could come with you, but you know how it is.'

'I'd love to take you, mother, you know that. I'll read a bit, unwind, and I'll send you a card. *And* I'll come and see you for a weekend in November.'

'Promise?'

'Promise.'

'That's Uncle David calling for something. Well, what with the cost of calls and everything I'd better ring off. Love to you from us both, and God bless, darling.'

'Thanks. Bye, mother.'

James turned on some more lights. What a day! It started ages ago. He picked up some books and then put the kettle on. He stood watching it boil, warming his hands on the gas. Mother: that wasn't much fun. Still, Helen was; a very good day. He stirred the coffee slowly and took it through; it was nice to be back in his flat. Eleven-fifteen. He'd never be able to sleep, not for an hour or two.

Perhaps he'd push his way through a pile of work, those fourth form essays – he'd be as generous and encouraging as possible; no more of this carping. That outburst against Alan, really! His red biro worked away. Yes, good idea but develop it. Eight weeks and he still hadn't made the effort to see them at home. Oh, spelling, come on, you can write more interestingly and accurately than this. Eight weeks of being tied up with himself. No, not exactly. And Helen and Tom. Your paragraphing is weak but you have an exciting imagination. Two months of peevish silliness, getting all worked up about the Secular Saint. He'd given more time to Tom than Uncle David, more to Helen than mother – well, he had to live, didn't he? Well done, I look forward to reading more work like this. Paltry lies and evasions on the phone, sins of omission. He ought to have a hard look at himself.

He put the last book on the pile. Midnight. Not tired yet. Time for a letter.

Dear Uncle David,

This will not be a long letter. It is late at night and I have just been exceedingly well cudgelled by mother for not visiting you. It is, if anything, a letter to keep you in touch until I return from Wales.

Some days I experience more than I do in other years. I remember the first time I saw *Othello*, in the Church hall at Oakington – do you remember that? – I can recall every minute of the day, every breath in my body as I watched. What it was all about I didn't have a clue, but I wanted to discuss it with you. (We've always enjoyed discussing, haven't we? I often discuss things with you when you're not there.) Then there was a conversation I had on Reading railway platform with a terribly miserable man; it must be ten years ago now. He told me he was going to throw himself under a train, sooner or later. 'It might be today, it might be tomorrow, but I've had enough of all this,' he said. I can see him now, his tie pin and little moustache; I can see the way his eye accused me; I can taste the warm smell of the tea I bought him.

It seems as if today might have been one of those days. Please tell Mother I'm sorry about being so unhelpful on the phone. She puts me on the defensive, although I'm sure she doesn't mean to, and I obviously have upset her.

I'll see you before long.

Yours,
James.

One o'clock. He slipped into his going-to-bed routine. Wash up the bits left, breakfast laid, switches off. All that was needed was Helen in bed. Come on, clean your teeth, splash your face with cold water. Next week perhaps? Perhaps. He took off his clothes and sat on the bed thinking of the day, flicking through a book in his fingers. He lay back and read for a few moments. John le Carré,

Ian recommended it. But James couldn't follow the intrigue, the plot was too much for him, so he tried an A. E. Coppard story. Much better. His eyes began to fade. He took out his contacts and turned out the light, to be with her. His mind and body throbbed.

Only three days to go. Glad he'd written to Uncle David, he felt better. Letter. Oh, that letter by the door, he'd forgotten it. He turned the light on, got out of bed and went to the front door. He opened it. It was typed.

Blood filled his ears and cheeks. His tongue felt thick.

JAMES   BURNETT
JUST A BASTARD
JUST A BOOK –
          – WORM

Oh, Christ, no.

Chapter Fifteen

Thank goodness he didn't have to teach; well, if playing a tape was teaching, he was. He'd agreed to *The Seagull* because it was Chekhov, because it would make an interesting change, because it illustrated various themes which tied in with the love poetry, but mostly because it was easy to press a button. So, to ironic cheers, James dragged the old tape-recorder into his classroom. The Kiss of Death, the Physics Department called James, he blew up anything electrical by touching it. In his hands the *Othello* cassette fed on its own entrails. Tentatively, he tried *The Seagull*. It worked. 'Tonight our presentation is . . .' He stopped it and re-wound a fraction too much. The tape came off the end. He put it back in the hole.

'Sorry, everyone. I didn't sleep too well last night, writing and reading letters.' Don't look at him. 'Right, a few quick words on Chekhov before I play Act I.'

'Is the tape going to break down, sir?'

'At the moment, Dawson, the only thing likely to break down in this classroom is me, but thank you for your concern.' James played his own internal tape on Chekhov: he enjoyed listening to himself on this one. Now do notice the pauses, they're crucial, and the gaps in the dialogue, it's as if Chekhov is a composer, it's all part of the symphony of emotions. Now Trepliov and Trigorin, the young, aspiring writer and the established middle-brow. It's very moving stuff, at least I think so, but I hope you also find it funny, laughing with, not at. . . . He understands people so well, the fools, the successes, the selfish, the failures – all of us. I've read every play and short story many times, even the different translations, no I'm not bragging, Scott. If I could get a bust of Chekhov for this shelf I would, even at the risk of a chalk moustache, but the Russian Embassy isn't too keen on gentle pre-Revolution Russians. James stopped. Has anyone ever told you you're a boring book-worm? And a bastard?

'Sorry.' He pressed the machine and listened. For ten minutes or more he listened, entranced, as every man and woman, the essence of each, was caught, held and alive. Oh, the anguish of Trepliov, young love, even that awful play he'd written, how James felt for him, how he loathed Arkadina, the mother, for laughing at his gaucheness. 'There's no action in your play,' Arkadina was saying, 'it's all talk.' You bitch, you bloody bitch. Action? The action is inside us. Trepliov was now blubbering, shouting out the famous spiteful lines, 'honeying and making love in the nasty sty'.

He stopped the tape.

'What's that a quote from?'

'*Hamlet*,' three or four shouted. Obviously.

He regretted the schoolmasterly point but went on:

'Yes, Trepliov is a kind of Hamlet, isn't he, I suppose all young . . .' He started the tape. Nina was so silly, she was always saying things like, 'I think there ought to be love in a play', and then beginning to fall for Trigorin. She was such a twit, couldn't she see? The story, if there was one, developed with its endless comings and goings, a flux of pointless visits; nothing much seemed to happen, apart from the odd crisis, but then nothing much did happen, especially for poor Masha and her boring schoolmaster. The boys were laughing. Was Hopkins? Yes, a bit, but not enough to tell.

James looked at them all. Scott, Nigel, Hopkins, Dawson, Harvard. 'I feel touched by your love but I can't return it, that's all. Have some snuff.'

'Sorry to interrupt again, you laughed; quite, it is funny; and sad, absurd. Chekhov has an ear for the absurdities, the little dignities and indignities of our . . .'

He caught Nigel's eye: don't get too soft-centred, not a cosy chapel chat, sir, please, you're better than that. So for the rest of the lesson the tape ran. 'I'm telling you this because you're a writer,' Masha said. 'You can make use of it if you like.' Chekhov spoke to them all, and James and the boys experienced the joys and nourishment of literature; Uncle David's words were right – of life through a key-hole, of life at one remove, of life heightened.

After the bell three or four came up to his desk.

'Sir, when Trepliov lays the seagull at Nina's feet, what's he trying to say?'

'Is it that he knows he's had it?' Dawson suggested.

'Possibly,' James said, 'but it doesn't *have* to be all capital letters, all symbolic.'

'And that bit when Trigorin takes notes on the dead seagull, for a short story, what's Chekhov getting at? I'm a bit lost. Is it that he's trying to make us prefer Trepliov to Trigorin?'

'I don't know that it's a matter of preferring. They're two different men, that's all, two different ways of living.'

'Well, one of them is a mess and one's a cool guy.'

'Or one man's pain is another man's literature.'

They all laughed in admiration at Nigel's remark.

'Cheerio, sir, have a good half term. That was great, sir. Are we going on with it after half term?'

'Yes, yes of course. Thanks, I'm glad you liked it. And

yes, a very happy half term to you. See you next week.'

'Hope it never comes, sir!'

'I know what you mean.'

They drifted off.

'Sir?'

'Ah, Nigel, I'll be with you in one moment; unplug the lead for me, will you? Just a second while I fight this monster.' He put the lid on it, exaggerating his incompetence. 'Nigel, did you know Chekhov once threw out a house-guest, a famous visitor; he threw his trunk downstairs, and do you know why? He saw this man, some Count or other, walking down the garden path lopping the tops off the flowers, lopping them off with his cane. Threw him out, overcoat, cane, Count and all. Marvellous!'

Nigel nodded. 'That's how I feel about people like that,' he said, 'but I doubt that I'd throw them out.'

'I'm not sure I would either.'

'Could I have a word with you, sir, in private some time?'

'Of course. But I'm in a bit of a rush at the moment.' James put the tape-recorder in the cupboard under the window.

'Some time after half term, would that be all right, Nigel?' He turned. But the boy had gone.

James sat at his desk, marking as fast as he could; if he worked hard now on these third formers he'd have time for . . .

Tom walked in. 'Here he is, then, earning his money.' James did his I'm-too-engrossed-to-hear and Tom sat down loudly, banging a desk.

'Oh, sorry, didn't see you.'

'How about the George and Dragon for a change tonight?'

'Sorry, I'm very tied up with water voles and cascading

leaves at the moment.'

'See you there at nine.'

'It depends,' James said, pointing at the exercise books. 'Oh, all right, but it's not my favourite place: too much gin on the carpet and a penny on all beers.'

'Let's give it a go.'

There really were too many water voles sniffing around the tinkling streams under the burnished sun. 'I do not want master-pleasing essays,' he wrote on one, then scratched it out and put, 'Please write in a personal, direct way.'

From then on he ticked alternate paragraphs, thinking of the evening.

He hadn't been to the George and Dragon for a couple of years and it hadn't improved. If you liked cricket prints and brasses it wasn't too bad, and the purple and copper bar was tolerably anonymous pub-land. The people were the problem. Tom was already at the bar and handed James his drink.

'Cheers, you're right about the prices.'

'Cheers. Have a good trip to Edinburgh.'

'And you to Wales.'

They sat in the mauve railway compartment, facing each other, not feeling they had to talk just yet. Should he ask about Jenny again, or what Tom was now feeling about England on closer acquaintance, or mention the letter . . . could he talk about it, repeat exactly what it said? Perhaps when Tom had gone back James would write and tell him he'd made his term; he didn't think he could say it to his face.

Tom sipped his beer, savouring it on his lips.

'Oh, God,' James said, 'that's wrecked it.'

'What has?' Tom stirred himself.

'Two boys, over there with girls; I can't see who one

is but the other is that bloody boy Hopkins – trust my luck. And with the Hogan girls.'

'Does it matter?'

'Well no – well yes. I mean they're under age, it's against the school rules, and it isn't half term yet. And they know. Hopkins has the Evil Eye on me.'

'Will they go?'

'We'll have to see.'

Tom swung round to look at them.

'Those people they're with, the adults, haven't I met them? At Ian's party? Paul somebody?'

'Yes, the Hogans, Paul and Janet Hogan. Typical of them.'

The girls, all dressed up and ready, stood in magazine poses. Why didn't James insist they went to the Plough, then there would have been a quiet hour's drinking and talking (or not talking), no schoolmasterly problems and a nice run-in to half term with Helen. Instead, the Hogans and Hopkins: everything he disliked all rolled up in one package. Janet Hogan, mutton, was standing there, drinking, smoking, exuding no-generation-gap.

'What's he like, Paul Hogan?' Tom asked.

A property-dealer, he got old people out of their homes for cash settlement, a smart operator. James's stomach ticked.

'Well,' James said, 'in my opinion, and I am, as you know, Tom, given to understatement, he is a shit of hell. Another drink? They're obviously not leaving.'

James walked over to the bar and tapped the other boy on the shoulder. He swivelled round, reddening. It was Library Side-Kick. His shirt was open to mid-chest to show he wasn't a girl, with the regulation chain round his neck.

'I'm sorry, I don't know your name, but you'll have to

go. You're in the Lower Sixth aren't you?'

The boy nodded. One of the Hogan girls came up closer. The boy went redder. She had blonde hair, and smoked with deliberation.

'You mean I've got to leave, now? Can't I finish my drink?'

'Yes, do finish it, then go, if you wouldn't mind.'

The boy shrugged uncomfortably. The girl glared. She was good-looking and ugly.

'Two lagers, please,' James called over the girl's head to the barman. As he took out the money his hands were shaking.

'Thank you, thank you so much,' James said. As he looked back Side-Kick and high-lights were whispering to Janet Hogan, probably trying to extricate themselves. Hopkins had deliberately not yet turned round. Janet Hogan was standing, hands on hips, wearing tight trousers. Her bottom wasn't up to them. English mutton. She came over to James. James had a glass in each hand.

'Oh, this is all so silly,' Janet said, 'why on earth can't we all have a quiet civilized drink together? Aren't you schoolmasters ever off duty?'

'Good evening, I'm sorry, Mrs Hogan, but I think both boys should leave. Your daughters are of course your responsibility.'

Hopkins was now standing behind Janet, looking nasty. James felt one of the glasses being taken skilfully out of his right hand. Tom was there and he spoke in a very quiet unusual voice.

'I think Mr Burnett is right. They should go.'

'And who are you?' Janet flushed.

'I'm sorry,' James said, 'I thought you'd met at the Wilkins place in September. Mrs Hogan, Mr Newman. Mr Newman is over from Australia, teaching at the

College.'

'And what does this have to do with Mr Newman may I ask?' Janet was confident, standing on her gins, on her territory.

'You may ask,' Tom said. 'I'm teaching at the College. Mr Burnett just explained that.'

'But only since September.'

'Only since September, yes, but as they are paying me, and I am teaching people like that,' he pointed at Hopkins, 'and that,' he pointed at Side-Kick, 'I have a right to my view, and my view is that Mr Burnett is correct. They should leave.'

James wanted to look at Tom but daren't.

'Well, you listen to me, Mr Newman – '

'No, you listen to me, Tits and Make-Up . . .'

Beautiful, Tom.

'Tell your young men to leave or I'll throw them out.'

Oh, Tom Newman, *Paul* Newman, you beaut.

Janet Hogan's mouth was quivering, creasing into older lines. 'I beg your pardon . . . you're telling me . . . you're standing there and telling me they've got to leave . . .'

Paul Newman nodded. Chew a match-stick, Tom, please. This town ain't big enough for You and Tits. James's mouth was dry. He wanted to drink but couldn't move his hand. Everything, as they say, stopped. Paul Hogan was pretending to talk to another man. Under the brasses and cricket prints other discreet English eyes were watching the colonial scene, not hearing it, but knowing it. Janet drew in a breath, moved away and talked rapidly to the girls and boys. They bent closer to listen. As Tom and James walked back towards their first-class compartment, Paul Hogan, all heartfelt insincerity, came across, his hands caressing the air.

'Look, there's no need for all this, surely. We've made

a silly mistake and I'm sorry, I really am, if we've embarrassed you chaps on your patch, but I must say, Mr Newman, you haven't done much tonight for your country. I didn't really believe you Australians were as loud and brash as rumour has it, but it seems you are. Let's have no more of this, shall we, let's call it a day. Perhaps it would be best if we both apologized.'

'No way,' Tom said. 'I spoke very quietly to your wife. I doubt you could have heard what I said. Ask her to tell you.'

James sat down, he couldn't look up. He wanted to lie on the carpet among the gin stains and roar. He sniggered into his beer. With Tom he could take anything, phone calls, poison letters, anything.

'Paul, we must leave,' Janet said, pulling his elbow, 'this *minute*, Paul.'

Ever so fractionally ruffled, Paul Hogan put down his drink.

Hopkins looked straight at James. (What next?)

Janet led them all out, mock-dignified, burning, sheepish, surly. Tom watched them go, rubbed his hands together at a job well done, and sat down. Some beer ran down the inside of James's nose.

'Unbelievable,' he coughed.

'Oh, Jeez, James, I'd had enough of your nice-nasty footsy-footsy. With cows like that it's time for the dung-and-debris approach.'

'She was livid, wasn't she, God she was furious. Do you think he heard what you called her?'

'If he didn't he'll never know.'

They laughed and drank and wiped their eyes.

'Oh boy, oh boy.'

He'd tell him now.

'Tom, I didn't tell you but I've also had a poison pen letter. Yesterday. I think it was Hopkins – I saw it just now in his eyes.'

Tom looked at the door through which Hopkins just left.

'I'll fix that bastard.'

'You think it's definitely him?' James said.

'I know it's him,' Tom said.

'How do you know, have you heard something?'

'Just leave him to me.'

'Tom, what comes after a poison pen letter?'

'Nothing.'

Tom suddenly laughed, and said, 'Do you think they'll report me to Head? I haven't had my final salary cheque yet.'

'No, they haven't got a leg to stand on.'

They finished their drinks and left. As they walked up the main street to the Plough, James wanted to put his arm round Tom, but they had to pass the College. And after all. . . .

Chapter Sixteen

Soon, when he was off the M4, James would be happier. Out of bed at five-thirty, he'd picked Helen up at six, and at times he'd found the long stretch a strain on his eyes. Smelling of tooth-paste, Helen jumped into the Mini quite cheerfully, but by the time they were through London, already tense with traffic, Helen's eyes were closed. He kept looking at her. Teaching had worn her out. Days after the nervous energy was switched off the exhaustion caught up with you; she'd been on holiday for nearly five days before James, but she was drained pale.

The car moved across the rolling, flattening plains of England; to left and right, Stonehenge, Oxford, Marlborough, the Cotswolds. James steadily moved past lanes of lorries, thinking of England, of Tom, of Scotland – would he be in Princes Street, or finding a room, or booking a ticket for the Traverse Theatre? Helen slept on. Although he'd have liked the company he was glad she could sleep safe and sound while he drove; he poured his feelings into her and she couldn't say no; something was held between them, no one else was in on this.

When he stopped at the Severn Bridge to pay the toll, Helen murmured, what's the time, ten-thirty, be there in an hour or two, go back to sleep. James leant across her and turned the radio on softly. Lucky girl to be able to sleep in a car, he wished he could; lucky me to have Helen, no, to be with Helen. The Mini moved slowly up the bridge, as it arched strong and clear from England to Wales – not quite Wales, but it felt like that. Suddenly the music was too loud, the reception was so clear up here. A querulous wavering voice cried: we're changing day to day, but tell me, where do the children play? He turned if off and looked down on the broad, filmy mud flats of the estuary. The car carried on over the long bridge, carrying James miles from the College and boys, to a country cottage for a weekend with Helen. He started humming. Two suitcases and my love to keep me warm. Corny songs. If the weather held it would be good, walking over the hills, and even if it poured, if on the top of the mountain the rain ran in tiny streams down her face, she'd splutter and laugh. What if things went wrong? Things did go wrong, they did all the time. Hadn't all the reading, the years of books taught him that? If not, if it was not true, why was one always expounding on Shakespeare's tragedies, on Sophocles, or *Middlemarch*? You could always draw up another list, all comic and humorous writers, but by and large they weren't as good, one's mind didn't live in them. And those smart comic novels written by Bright Wide-Awake Young Things, with endless pages of trendy sex; what did they leave you with? Nothing.

He looked at Helen. The fall of the skirt on her thighs. Look up, careful. Turn-off coming up, number twenty-five. They'd make it by lunch time; things would be quieter now. A coffee would be nice. Well, too bad, she's asleep. Gradually, as the mountains appeared in the distance, the countryside began to lose its English arrangedness; at the end of every lane and dotted along the road were grey houses with grey-white walls and slate roofs.

Tonight. What about the sleeping arrangements? It was important they were right. Mother said there was one bed, a single obviously; he had a camp bed in the boot and on the back seat a sleeping bag. Wouldn't most girls have asked? She could look after herself. Or perhaps she took life in her stride and wasn't interested in such calculations? He put the Mini into a long left-hand bend. Helen slipped off his shoulder; he held the bend steadily, carefully passing two or three cars. Little seemed to be going their way. Now there were end-of-autumn trees; the last leaves were flicking off them, faded ochre leaves which lightly clipped his windscreen. One clung to the wipers. Ten miles or more, twenty minutes, and they'd be there, hidden away in the hills. Helen half opened her eyes, sat up, turned the rear-view mirror towards herself, said God and slumped again. James adjusted it slowly back to suit himself: catching his eyes he tried a craggy-I-drive-on-in-the-blizzard-while-the-others-collapse. It failed.

There were only five or six buildings in Pentrefan, not really a village, just a place. There are such places; you can only call them by their names. The first thing you saw was the Chapel, a Welsh Methodist barn which stood where the roads parted; on it the grey plaster face was badly cracked and lumps bulged out, swollen by dampness. The mud coating of the lane was spattered with earlier plaster fallings. Across the way a white gate led down to a farm. Chickens and dogs moved in and out of the half-open door. Up the other road – it wasn't easy to tell if anyone lived there – was a yellow crumbling building. Planks slipped out of the roof. Wherever James and Helen walked they could hear the river, a thin fast mountain stream. A few cows squelched around the edge.

From halfway up the road above the cottage the most striking feature was the graveyard, a field close to the chapel, full of old appropriate stones and new portly slabs standing haphazardly on the slope. Despite the formal rusty railings at the front it was no more than a rough field for the dead.

The waste ground around James's place was covered with blocks and empty cement bags; they had to step over old bricks and ruts to get to the front door. James was delighted with its unpretentious, solid atmosphere. It was ready for warmth, it was small and square, the kind of house any kind of man might live in. He walked round quickly, looking at everything downstairs. Now upstairs. Two bedrooms. He could hear Helen coming up behind him; she popped her head round the door. There was one old bedstead, a single; the other bedroom was empty.

In the kitchen Helen said, 'The fireplace is super, isn't it? You're lucky to have the use of this place, aren't you?'

'Yes, with some carpets and chairs it'll cheer up.'

'A fire is the best thing – is there any wood?'

'Look, let's push off in the car to a pub, there must be one, get a bite if we can, then go for a walk to get some wood. Are you still tired?'

'No, I'm sorry about that. No, I'd love a walk.'

At the door James turned and looked at it all: the long stone fireplace, the small windows, the staircase, and through the kitchen window the fields beyond. This would do nicely, very nicely. Outside a farmer was patiently urging his horse up the hill.

'Excuse me,' James called, 'is there a pub around here?' The farmer stopped, then carefully side-backed his horse, pace by pace. He touched his cap to Helen. His face was weathered florid.

'Yes, indeed there is, yes. Up there, about two mile.'

'Thanks.'

'Only one, see, can't miss it, very good, very friendly.

Is this your place then, we was wondering you know whose it was, like?'

'Well, yes it is.'

He smiled down, not keen to move on.

'Very nice too, yes. You wouldn't be from round 'ere, then?'

'No, we're from the London area, south east really.'

'Yes, England. I thought so.'

They all smiled at each other.

'Well, I must be going on, can't spend all day here, now can I? Must get up on the top, see how things are with my lot, see. Lovely views up there, if that's what you like. Nice to see you, might see you later.'

'I hope so,' Helen said.

The check cap was touched again, and he worked his horse, 'C'mon now, Chess, *Diawch*, c'mon, on up the road with you.' He paused to turn and wave after fifty yards or so. They got into the Mini.

'Great bloke,' James said as he started it up.

'Mm.'

'He didn't seem one of those gloomy R. S. Thomas types.'

'You and your types.'

He drove up into the hills.

James banged his head on the door as he went in but liked the landlord, the beer and the cheese. They were certainly going back in the evening.

'None of the ghastly passing traffic lot here,' he said to Helen.

'What are we then?'

'Locals.'

Although the drink and the open fire was making them tender and sleepy they were determined to 'earn it' before they returned in the evening. You couldn't be in the

Welsh hills and not walk; if the afternoon was spent fighting the wind and cold cheeks until you glowed through, the evening would be better. They put on their anoraks and walked the car and the pub out of their legs. Stopping every now and then to point out a huddle of buildings or for a breather, suddenly they were there on the top. 'Pan-or-am-ic.' The top wasn't a mountain, more a high plateau, marvellous for striding out. James took a folded map out of his pocket and made Helen laugh with his pronunciation of the names.

'Or whatever you call it, then. You say it if you're so clever.' They looked round and at each other. Apart from clumps of low bushes and the wild ponies there was nothing: a whole world of their own. Will these always be great things, great things to me?

'Not even a shepherd,' James said, 'no one.'

Ponies munched in packs, then shuffled and pounded off, ten, fifteen, twenty of them, their manes flying, to another place. James and Helen sauntered a few paces over the coarse, springy grass; it was lumpy, as if millions of moles had humped up only to retire just before they broke through. James turned Helen round a full circle.

'Let's run to that post over there.'

'Where? Which one?'

'Just there, along my arm, can't you see, and then drop down to the car. Shouldn't take too long. I'll race you.'

She bounded over the earth, earth sprung with mountain rain, while he took up a canny second position, waiting for the tactical burst. Might be fun to trip her. Damn the girl, he had a race on his hands, he felt his shoes and socks digging; what the hell, she could run. He sucked in breath, pulled up with her, elbowed her into a large lump and just won. They leant against the post.

'You didn't tell me you were a muscley athlete,' James panted.

'Oh, I like that!'

Neither wanted the afternoon to end, until the light dimmed and inched off the hills. And then they came down, keeping to the line of the wall, a hill country wall, grey stone balanced on grey stone, held together by skill, irregular and firm, natural and timeless.

A sheep dog lay by the door. At the bar some were speaking English, some Welsh, and some a mixture. The locals and the visitors were conscious of each other, as strangers are. In the corner of the living room where James and Helen sat – it could hardly be called a bar – the landlord was knocking up an announcement about the Ystrad Darts League. A row of farmers and shepherds stood around, grouped conspiratorially, talking fast. They wore wellingtons or leather boots, flat caps and brown or green jackets; they all smoked, with knobbed heavy hands, and without looking, returned their glasses to the same spot each time, never spilling a drop up or down. Their natural uniformity intrigued James, even their laughter was communal, each man's stories or asides were generously received.

Two younger men, probably not eighteen but they weren't boys, played quoits, shooting shy glances at Helen as they put up the score. Helen looked at her shoes: how expensive, they embarrassed her, and her furry coat felt silly. James's hands were so white. They glanced at each other, excluded. James looked at his watch; only nine-thirty, they were not ready to return to the house.

'Do you think the fire is safe?' James asked.

'Yes, I should think so.'

James went to the counter. A man, in the same mould

as the others, came in and stepped over the sleeping dog. As he greeted everyone he saw Helen.

'Hullo there, you again. Did you have a good walk?'

'Yes thanks. It was lovely. We went up to the top as you suggested.'

'Can I get you a drink, please?' James said. 'I'd like to.'

'Very nice of you, yes, a pint please. But look you should be having it on me. And look at them,' he raised his voice, 'look at you, boys, damn unfriendly. *Duw*, *Duw*, what kind of welcome is this, mm?'

James looked down and went for the extra pint.

'Here they are, this lady and man, miles away from London and what are we doing; all we is doing is talk, I tell you.'

James sat down next to Helen, sharpened by this welcome.

'Do you think, do you think it's right, having a place over here? The man was being very friendly but they see us as outsiders, a threat, we don't belong and we never could – like that trendy priest who lands on that lonely island, you know that book, to tell the out of-date-monks, you know the . . .'

'I haven't read it,' Helen said, leaning forward. She thought for a bit then said, 'It wouldn't be easy to belong here, not for a good while, you'd have to earn their friendship. They're bound to be on the defensive.'

James looked at the men. One left the room unsteadily, lifting his feet slightly higher than he need have done.

'And anyway, James, you aren't very friendly to people. You tend to like only a few people.'

'I like only a few people a lot.'

Two pints later, one of the other men raised his glass to Helen.

Slowly, with the merest touch of shyness, all of them

started to sing, a sound rising from the well of their community, all taking parts as if they'd spent the afternoon, not on the hills, but in rehearsal. It was their habit. As the tenors, the glamour boys, hit the top notes they looked up proudly, red in the face, while the sound and modest basses studied their wellingtons. Everyone sang, except James and Helen; behind all this the landlord dried glasses, wiped the bar and lent a hand to the basses. The conspiring friendly atmosphere became, for a moment, one open to the heart; a kind of beauty touched the room. At the end a few nodded approval in their warm beer but the others shook their heads. *Diawl*, no no, that wouldn't do, boys, no no. Nowhere near. Another man, one of the tenors this time, filled up their pints – it seemed they took it in turns behind the bar; were they all trusted?

Suddenly, without a sign, they started again, caught as if in an old photograph, all weight on elbows on the bar, one boot crossed over the other.

'I wish I could understand the songs,' Helen said. 'They're very moving.'

Released by the warm fire James wanted to hold her hand; this was the moment to say I think I love you, no I *know* I love you (I want you). He held back. This was masculine country, you couldn't hold her hand in here.

A very English-looking man came in. He seemed half-known; some nods.

'A pint, please, and do you mind if I bring my dog in here?' he said, too close to squire for comfort.

'Yes yes, as long as he's well behaved.'

'Well behaved? Good Lord, he's better behaved than I am,' the Englishman chortled at his unspeakable past.

'Well, send the dog in and stay outside yourself then,' one of the tenors said, handing him his drink.

Everyone laughed. 'Very good, I like that,' the Englishman said, and drank an uncomfortable pint.

Soon they'd better get back to the cottage. The fire would surely be out. And for ten minutes James had been praying to God they wouldn't ask him to lead 'D'ye ken John Peel' or some idiot song by way of contributing a little bit of England; unlikely, of course, but once he'd thought of it James itched to be off.

He looked at Helen.

> May I touch said he
> How much said she

Damn that poem, intrusive little thing

> A lot said he
> Why not said she

Writing affectedly cool poems was one thing; boys did that very well in magazines, but handling a girl like Helen was quite another. Sex wasn't cool.

'I think we probably ought to go and check that fire.'

'Yes, all right,' Helen said, 'but I like it here. I could listen to them sing all night, couldn't you?'

James nodded and took the glasses back to the bar. Helen stood up. They wished her and James a genial, inscrutable good-night.

'*Nos da, pob hwyl.*'

'Good-night,' James called.

He lifted the latch, ducked his head and guided Helen out into the dark.

They drove through the winding lanes and the hedges were close so he had to concentrate.

They parked just beyond the cottage; as they walked back they heard their footsteps. The place did take some warming up. The fire had gone fairly low and the stark light of the naked bulb, the lack of comfort, oppressed James. While James stoked it up, raking out the cinders, Helen made some coffee; James became voluble, trying to fill the lack. It was all too quiet, they should have stayed till closing time (if there was one); he should have brought his radio.

'It feels a bit damp in here,' he called through. Some whisky, too, might help.

'Oh, it's all right,' she said, clinking the spoons on the mugs.

He looked in the kitchen. Her back was to him.

'How are you getting on in there?'

'Fine thanks.'

'Would you like a whisky with it?'

'No thanks, but you go ahead. Just coffee for me.'

He took out his pencil torch, the bottle was under the sleeping bag on the back seat. He fumbled under it, pulled out the bottle, and took it back to the kitchen. He half filled the only small glass there, filled it with water and went into the main room. Helen was crouching by the fire. James put off the main light, leaving only the small one on; he sat next to her.

'Shall I make up your bed for you down here? I can fetch the mattress down when you're ready and you can put your sleeping bag on top; it'll be drier.'

Helen smiled into her coffee.

'Yes, that would be fine. I am a bit sleepy.'

'All right, I'll do that then.'

James groped his way upstairs and found the room with the bed. He pulled the mattress slowly down, step by step, and across the bare boards.

'Let me help you,' Helen said, pulling one end. They placed it in front of the fire.

'Damn this fire, it's not right yet,' James said, 'I love fires though.' He gave a little laugh and sat on the mattress, kicking a log with his foot. Helen drank her coffee. He lifted the slowest burning log with a stick and the flames licked round it.

'I enjoyed that pub, didn't you? They drink but they don't get belligerent – we might pop up there tomorrow, what do you think?'

'Yes, if you'd like to; it was nice.'

'Yes, it's been a good day altogether, hasn't it, mm?'

He put his arm round her, touching her shoulders and the side of her breasts. He pulled her to him. They lay together, the light of the fire revealing their faces. James kissed her. She put one of her long hands on her knee.

'Sure you wouldn't like some?' James said, as he lay on his arm, drinking a little whisky.

'No thanks. I must have had too much to drink at the pub: I feel so sleepy.'

He felt her shoulder against him.

'James, I'm very tired, it's been a super day, the walk and everything, but I really don't think I can keep awake.'

He lay very still. Then he said, 'Oh, OK, fine, fine, I'll get your sleeping bag shall I, and the camp bed?'

'Yes, please, if you would. I'm sorry I forgot to bring it in, it's on the back seat.'

'Is it? Right.'

He took his torch and again went out into the dark.

James looked across the room.

'I've got to just write a couple of cards and then we'll go out, shall we?'

'Yes, I'd like to,' Helen said, engrossed, and went on reading.

'I won't be long.'

'There's no hurry, I could read by this fire for hours.'

James picked up his biro, chewed it, and wrote

Dear Maggie,

I'm in Wales and thought you might like this post-card of the mountain ponies. And look at the mountains in the background! The ponies run free all over the hills. They are very beautiful but not very friendly. When I come back I'll come and see you and take you for a walk. It's a long time since I read to you. Lots of love to you from Wales, and to Peter, Philip and Anna.

(Uncle) James.

He picked up another card and then wrote

Wales, November 2nd. Dear mother and Uncle David,

Helen stretched across to the other side of the mattress to pick up her coffee. She sipped it, then rolled over on to her back.

If he wrote very small he'd get a lot on.

Well done: you've made a marvellous buy. It's perfect. I got up early this morning to get the fire going and I'm now sitting by it looking out at the countryside. It's quite cold today but, like the people, the place is full of character. Last night I went to the local pub – full of singing Welshmen, too good to be true! – and then read far into the night.

The builders have done a very thorough job; there is very little mess. The kitchen equipment is all in. I'm not sure what I'll do today but there's plenty of interest around here. There's a feeling of being miles away from everywhere. The leaves have all gone, over there are the mountains, I feel quite Wordsworthian. I'll give you all the details when I see you.

Lots of love, James.

Hope you can read this!

'I think I saw a post box down by the main junction,' James said, 'I'll go and pop these in. Do you have anything to send?'

'No thanks.'

They should have brought some more bread and fruit: he felt quite empty inside. The air was chill on his face. Dropping down the slope he found his feet breaking into a jog trot along the river. Yes, the air was certainly colder. He steadily built up his pace, urging himself on. It was like those cross countries at school when you disliked the pressure in your chest and liked the challenge; his feet banged their way past some low rubble walls, past a low-roofed house. A woman looked up from scrubbing her step, her big arms bare to the elbow; a little boy watched her, sucking his thumb. On he ran, past the quiet wet fields, trodden by a few heavy cattle, and there it was, the post box, so small, set into a wall. They didn't write much round here. James laughed scornfully at himself. He leant against the wall hearing himself gather his breath, and slipped the card into the slit. Slowly he turned up the road, and as he walked back to the house the sweat dried on his back.

By lunch time Helen had finished her Margaret Drabble and was very quiet. James suggested a drive.

They drove round the lanes and time passed. They came up behind a line of stationary cars. James had to brake hard, barely finding enough room to squeeze past. Bits of rough overhanging hedgerow scratched the roof and side windows. It was something to talk about.

'How odd; what do you think it's all about?' Helen asked.

'I don't know, could be a rally. Unlikely though. No, look at some of these old bangers.'

'What, then?'

'There must be a pub around,' James said. 'The Welsh are always at the pub.'

'So are you.'

She was leaning forward, trying to work it out, her brown curly hair falling forward. Sara peered like that, but she'd be chattering more. But I don't want Sara here. When you parted from someone you took her along, for the ride, always there; like a painting in the spare room, it has to find a place somewhere.

'There must be a hundred cars at least,' she said.

'No, more I think. It's quite intriguing, I wonder what it can be,' he went on emptily, 'I really can't think.'

After the next corner the road opened out to reveal grey and white houses. On a high exposed spot there was a large square chapel.

'Shall we stop for a minute?' Helen asked.

'Why? Aren't there enough people here already?'

'Please, I'd like to.'

'All right.'

James drove beyond the last car and backed up close to a rusty iron gate. The wind was flattening down the grass and pulled at the half-open car door.

'Here, take your coat,' James said as she got out.

'No thanks, I'll be all right as I am.'

James looked up at the chapel roof with the grey clouds blowing past. The wind was even stronger than on his run. He followed Helen up the muddy, grass path. He felt very conscious of his hands and feet. Already, in that strange random way, James sensed this would be one of those moments: why are we walking to see this, and who will decide if it slips out or is gummed in the book?

They got to the top of the rise. The women were in black or grey, the men in black. Every corner and edge was full; there must have been two or three hundred people. It was like a film. The priest spoke quietly into the ground, in Welsh. James and Helen stood decently apart. As the singing started, a theatrically sad atmosphere held them all. Film, theatre, James was ashamed of his thoughts and turned away to look back at the chapel and up at the leadening sky. But he was right, his instincts were right: here, whatever the place was called, someone was leaving the stage, and why, in God's name, do it with canned music and closing crematorium curtains. Here, for hundreds of years, they had buried their friends and enemies in this way, and this was how they'd do it now. The priest spoke again, quietly, for many minutes. Then four men, with old ropes, lowered the box into a black oblong hole. James and Helen hurried back to the car. It was now very cold.

Chapter Seventeen

'Was she beautiful or not beautiful?' The words had been niggling away at him all evening; which novel began like that? He'd had enough and once he'd decided he wanted to go, the evening was a drag, and still on and on Marjorie was talking, in one of her Sincere Replies Only moods.

'But, Tom, don't you find us rather grey? Apparently visitors to England usually do, gracious but grey, snug but smug, that's how we're seen, apparently.'

'No, I like you a lot,' Tom said, 'I keep on saying it.' He drank some wine. 'It's true. Would you prefer it if I didn't like the English?'

James would prefer it if they'd all finish their cheese, then he could talk to Liz. Tom was uncomfortable, as unwilling to define the English (now that he knew their ways) to their face, as he was unsure (now that he'd been away a couple of months) of his Australian identity. Marjorie pushed on, dammit she almost sounded like Alan Priestley tonight; what was wrong with the woman? Why didn't she talk about Scotland, as Tom clearly wanted, or books? Presumably she didn't rate Tom on books: he wasn't English.

'So, we're not too coolly superior and class-ridden, fine, but don't you feel our political system needs a radical reform? Wasn't your Prime Minister saying something like that the other day?' Marjorie sat back, lips pursed, waiting for advice from the New World.

'Our Prime Minister,' Tom said, 'is the biggest Philistine since Goliath.'

'You read Bernard Levin too,' Ian said; which was rather good for him, and stood up as if the line was obviously conclusive. 'Let's go through.'

'That was a lovely meal, Liz, thanks,' James said. 'It's softened the blow of getting back to work. It's only a few days since the break but it feels an age.'

'I'm sorry Helen couldn't come; next time perhaps.'

'She was sorry too; she had to go to London. Hey, Liz, come and talk to me when you've got a moment; I can't take any more of Marjorie. She'll get on to books, which means me, in a moment.'

'Of course I will – I'll be over in a minute.'

Slightly turning his chair, James sat on his own near the fire, yawning; he didn't want to talk. 'Was she beautiful or not beautiful?' Was it a George Eliot?

He overslept the first morning back from Wales, perhaps worn out with the driving, went to school unprepared and empty inside, and – as he deserved – had to stomach classes of clock-watching boys. James looked at them looking at him. Break was too matey for words; and the first period afterwards he had a row with the Lower Sixth who were in just the right mood for a You'll be sulky I'll be surly struggle. The routine was simple: in a sarcastically accepting way James implied he didn't expect them to know much and they encouraged him by pretending to know even less, so they read *Death of a Salesman* as badly as they could while his mind dropped through Wales, the hills, the mattress, the pub, the silver-grey film of water under the Severn Bridge, and into a depression. Somehow he dragged his mind back to the bleary, pasty rows in front of him. No doubt about the sort of weekend this lot had, all beers and bras. They looked as if they'd had their fill.

Even Tom seemed low in the Common Room, reading magazines, and then, worst of all, his mother rang up for the details, as promised on your lovely card, of the Welsh trip, and as he clearly wasn't likely to go down there or ring she thought it best if she did the ringing. There was no one to talk to, except perhaps Liz, and then Marjorie prattled away and ruined this evening; even now she was going on.

'Are you an existentialist, then?' she asked Tom.

'No, I'm drunk,' he said.

Ian liked that so gave Tom another brandy. 'Oops,' Tom said.

'Was she beautiful or not beautiful?' *Daniel Deronda*? Yes, wasn't it? Anyway, so what.

Helen. One minute he was sure: when he was shaving, when he put the car away, while reading a poem; one minute he wasn't, the word was too big. One minute he had that knotted pain of recognition, the yearning for the next meeting, the touch of her hand; the next minute he doubted it all. It hadn't somehow fitted together, it was like a collection of short stories. The brown envelope was nice, though.

The only good thing since half term had been the teaching. The special class really took to *The Seagull*, and next week they wanted to discuss it and bring some love poems they liked. Even though he was still too prone to under-cut by apologizing, he felt a growing relationship with them, especially Nigel ('he thinks you're the best teacher he's got' – how often he said that to himself – thank you, Nigel, and Helen for telling me), and so far Hopkins (if it was) hadn't made his next move.

Just before he left tonight he heard the letter box. He'd rushed out, in his shirt and pants, from the bedroom expecting to catch Hopkins; he heard footsteps running downstairs, felt he couldn't follow, and ripped open the letter.

Dear James,
Thank you for Wales. I'm doing a painting for you. Sorry I couldn't come tonight; I've rung Liz to apologize.
Love, Helen.
I'll return the novels when I next see you.

He put the letter on his window-sill while he put on his trousers and tie, then re-read it. When he went out he propped it by his bedside table. She'd never written to him before.

Poor Tom. Marjorie wasn't his type. Tom looked at James and raised a why-doesn't-this-ex-varsity-tit-shut-up eyebrow at him. Tom. He'll be gone in a month or so, back to Jenny. Who was she, what was she like?

'Here I am,' Liz said, 'sorry to be so long.'

'I've just been to Scotland,' Tom said loudly to Marjorie.

'Ah, Scotland.'

What was more he intended to talk about it. He trod all over Marjorie with Edinburgh, Stirling and, on the way down, York Minster. James and Liz smiled as Tom opened out with reminiscence; he took in the whole room, relaxing into the world of anecdote, where you leave out the bad moments, colour the good, and flavour with alcohol.

'Liz,' James began quietly, 'what do you think of Helen?'

'I like her very much, more each time I see her.'

'So do I.'

'And mad, of course, if she doesn't grab you.'

'Ahh!'

'All the nicest girls are dying to know you.'

'You may remember that Sara was dying to know me.'

'Yes, Sara,' Liz said steadily into the fire. Footprints led towards the past, but they let them go. 'You always run yourself down, James. You mustn't.'

'Do I?'

'Yes, you do. I adore you for it, in a way, but don't overdo it.'

'I won't.'

'Are you as busy as ever, Ian is.'

'Mm, I suppose so, but nothing like as busy as you are. How do you do it? What's it like having children? I mean I know it's hard work and all that. If I had brothers and sisters I suppose I'd understand better. Do you feel you've got anything left, for yourself?'

'Oh, in many ways, yes. I mean I can't move freely and I can't concentrate for long and I can't dash off to Wales for lovely weekends, but Ian's a great help. He takes so much pressure off me.'

'Yes, I can imagine. He's like that in the department, always helpful. He lets me do what I want to. Tom says the same, he's never felt so free. Giving us our heads, I think that would be the phrase.'

'He thinks the world of you.'

'What's Maggie up to, what's she reading?'

'Everything. She's driving Mrs Peacock mad at school. She grabs every book, and this morning there was havoc – she ran round the classroom, knocking over this and that, no one knew what was going on. So Mrs Peacock, quite rightly, smacked her, which led to the fact that there was a crocodile on the floor. Mrs Peacock told her to stop it and apparently the crocodile has since eaten up Mrs P. Maggie buried her tonight, under the trees in the garden.'

'Lovely girl, she really is. That's decided it. I'm coming to see her tomorrow, if I may.'

'She'd love that. Your card really was sweet, it's by her bed. Tell me about Wales, it looked idyllic. What did you get up to?'

'You must come over some time, you'd like it.'

'Oh you wouldn't want us over there.'

'I would.'

There was a loud laugh across the room. Liz smiled.

'Tom seems to have enjoyed his half term. Having people from other countries is a breath of fresh air, isn't it? They make us see things differently.'

'Yes, I agree, they do.'

Chapter Eighteen

The moment he woke up he knew he was ill. James forced his eyes open. The back of his throat felt stapled together, pulling to open; his legs were leaden and dead and as he tried to sit up the weight of his brains rolled. It was ten to six. Whatever he'd got was bad. He lay there sweating into his sheets until seven-thirty, when he rang Ian and croaked he couldn't make it today.

'Nothing you ate here, I hope?'

'No, of course not.'

He put the phone down, wanting to be sick, but when he got to the bathroom he couldn't. He drank a cup of water, each swallow cracking his throat, and stumbled back to bed. A few hours later the door bell rang through his head. He got there, his pyjamas clinging to his legs.

'James, get straight back into bed,' Liz said, 'and we'll work out what you need.'

'Nothing, thanks Liz.'

'Into bed. We've obviously poisoned you.'

'Don't be silly.'

She followed him in.

'Lucozade, grapes, some juice. Yes?'

He nodded and swallowed.

'Any books? Another paper? Yes, but you will. You might want to read later. Now give me the key. Anyone who wants to get in can look under the mat.'

'I don't want to see anyone.'

He slept. When he woke in the afternoon she'd been back. The side table was covered with bottles and fruit, novels, the *Guardian* and a note. 'Dr Sinclair is calling at tea-time.' James changed his pyjamas. The doctor told him he had what everyone had and it could be a week. No, it wasn't 'flu – it was the virus going round. He'd be back in a day or two. James hoped he'd forget.

He lay there half asleep, his mind and blood wildly on Helen and Liz; he ran his hands on their arms and shoulders, legs, hair, into them, feeling them open, slow and hot. He sat up and drank some water. Friends of his, Oxford friends, had fallen in love with intelligent girls who moved from being stylish undergraduates into stylish jobs (writing features for newspapers) into stylish mothers in Battersea, into more mature stylish mothers in Bristol or Sevenoaks, moving on their competent journeys. Or so it seemed. Whereas he . . .?

Over the next few days of pills and dampness he got to know Helen's body; like Leda she floated above him naked, when he touched her skin she came down; he watched her draw herself naked, in the mirror, and when he said it was good she turned and he saw her back in the reflection. And, relentlessly, among these, he dreamt the usual ones, killing a man on a train, always the same man, yet never identifiable, and Maggie in a car crash outside Liz's gates, and he saw Helen and Liz running towards him and their hard, athletic bodies, familiar and strange, held him and he held them. He woke up, crying, running his hands through his damp hair. The front door bell rang and then he heard feet and the door knocked.

'James, how are ya?'

'Tom, pull up a chair.'

'How are you, eh?'

'Getting better, up in a few days I think.'

'Don't rush it for Christ's sake – there's no point. Ian

and I are covering most of your lessons, making them work for the first time.'

James smiled. Teaching seemed far away. Tom walked across to the window, his burly back cut out most of the light.

'How's Jenny?'

He half turned round.

'Fine.'

'I've never even seen a photo of her – do you have one?'

'Of course, yeah.' He looked through a few, tucked them back, before coming across with one to James's bed. She was quite tall next to him, attractive, smiling. Difficult to say more.

'Thanks. She's beautiful, isn't she? Sit down. Get yourself a beer from the fridge.'

Tom took the photo back, looked at it briefly, and said, 'Thanks, I'd like to, but I've got to go. See you tomorrow.'

There was another knock on the door.

'Come in. Hello, Nigel.'

'I'm sorry, sir, but the front door was open and I assumed . . .'

'Yes, that's right, come on in. Mr Newman's just going.'

'I'm not interrupting, am I?'

'See you, James, cheers Nigel.'

Nigel took off his duffel coat. He had on a polo neck sweater and jeans. He smiled nervously. He looked puffy and white, an over-worked adolescent.

'You don't look very. . . . I shan't stay long, sir, I wanted to see how you were.'

'Getting better. What are you up to in class?'

'Nothing much. When will you be back?'

Nigel picked up the Philip Larkin, something to do.

'Monday I hope. Have you read those?'

'Yes. They're very sad, aren't they; the ones I've read

are. There must be something better to write about than that?'

'They're disappointed, certainly, low key. Borrow it if you like. Some of them are very witty too, and . . . well, see for yourself.'

Nigel looked at the wall, dangling the Larkin in his hand.

'I see you do really have that quotation above your bed.'

'Why, didn't you believe me?'

James's head hammered. He'd already talked out what energy his dreams had left him. Nigel checked his finger-nails.

'How's that pretty girlfriend I saw you with a couple of weeks ago, up the other end of town?'

Nigel stirred and turned over a few pages, laughing in warning.

'It's all over. She's going out with someone else.'

He was very pale, with a low quietness in his manner.

'Oh, pity. You wouldn't like some coffee, would you?'

Nigel stared down. 'Yes, I would.'

Suddenly the boy got up and went into the kitchen. James called out instructions, hurting his throat. Nigel took a long time. How's that pretty girlfriend of yours! With all the things to talk about, what a stupid nosey way to start. Nigel came in with his coffee. James looked at him. Yes, he had been.

Between sips and stirs Nigel said, 'All those poems we've done, it's been great, the only good thing of the term. I really love those lessons. I try to write sometimes. I know what I'm trying to say but I can't "catch" it. Do you know what I mean?'

'Yes, I do.'

'And it's not as if I'm trying to say very much. I suppose that's partly what you were trying to say about Chekhov. I saw *Three Sisters* on TV. It was fantastic.'

He looked at James, his eyes strained, and went on: 'What do you think the point of it is, all this reading? I know you probably don't want to talk about it now, but I didn't want to ask in class in case you thought I was trying to get at you.'

'Mm. Well, I think reading's fun and interesting, for its own sake. And you also see into the world, perhaps a world you haven't experienced, perhaps can't experience. An imaginative key-hole.'

Nigel laughed.

'I know what you're thinking,' James said, 'but it's more than that. It's as if we're looking into our own secrets too, on a third ground, swimming in the rough sea but safe. There are a few mixed metaphors for you. With great books, don't you find you're opening out in your head, saying "Yes" to a new and better version of your life, well, your imaginative life.'

'I like that,' Nigel said, 'that's good. Can I tell you something?'

Yes, James nodded, but not too much.

'I've just done a ghastly thing. After tea, I tore up all her letters, all of them, and shoved them down the lavatory. And then I burnt her photograph. I took out my lighter and burnt her all up.'

Like the Hardy poem. Oh, for Christ's sake.

Nigel gulped some coffee, then warmed his hands round the cup.

'Oh, don't blame yourself too much. You felt you had to do something.' James then gave him his that's-the-way-it-goes smile.

'But have you ever done anything as sordid as that?' Nigel's eyes fastened on to James.

'Yes, often, but not as dramatic.'

'At first the bits wouldn't go away. I had to keep on flushing,' Nigel said, laughing and sniffling.

'Bloody typical, isn't it?' James said. He must ring her soon.

'That really pissed me off.' He took out his handkerchief and laughed a bit. 'Can I come and see you again? I feel miles away from College here, don't you?'

'Ex-actly.'

'Yes, you've got a nice place.' He pulled on his coat, his face still blotchy. 'Good-bye, sir.'

'Bye, Nigel, take the Larkin, might be just the thing! Next time I'll tell you what happened once to a schoolboy in a Spanish brothel.'

'You're joking!'

'I wish I was. Bye, Nigel.'

When he heard the front door click James pulled his legs out of bed. Perhaps some music. Radio 3. 'In this recording of Prokofiev's "Cinderella" . . .' He turned it off and wandered, distracted and weary, into the sitting-room. Rain smeared the window. Outside, the buildings across the street had faded into a black bank. He went back to the bathroom, brushed his teeth and washed his face. Now.

Holding the phone firmly, settling his voice with a cough, he dialled her number.

'Is that Helen?'

'Yes, is that James? James, I've just heard you're ill. Alan told me, after his lecture. What's wrong? How long have you been ill?'

'Not long, a few days. I just wanted to say I'm sorry I haven't been in touch . . . and thanks for the letter.'

'I'll come round and see you tomorrow.'

'No, no,' he put authority into his voice, 'I think that's a bad idea, thanks. The doctor says it's not advisable.'

'Oh, whatever you think best.'

'I'll ring you, when I'm back at school, and I wanted to say, about Wales . . . anyway I'll be in touch.'

'All right, James.'

Another day passed. Liz and Tom came, talking of this and that, before moving on.

'I want to squeeze as much as I can into the next month,' Tom said.

James dreaded their final parting.

'Before you go I must know what you really think of England, not like Marjorie, but I'd like to know.'

Tom was hearing but not listening. He didn't want to talk. He was doubtless thinking of April, preparing to leave James and England, withdrawing from affinity.

Chapter Nineteen

'The brothel. Come on, out with it.'

'What brothel?'

'The Spanish one. Oh come on, you were going to tell me.'

'What is all this? You've been reading too much David Niven. Or was I delirious at the time?'

'If you don't tell me you won't get the present I've brought you.'

'What present?'

'The brothel first.'

It was Friday night in the sitting-room. From the moment he'd woken up, wanting to be in bed with Helen, it had been a promising day.

Signalling a return to the fight he put on his shirt and trousers; later, Nigel cooked him an omelette, and although the whisky tasted acrid, probably interacting with the pills, James had drunk three glasses. The burning in his stomach was good, and he could feel more strength in his legs. He eased back on the chaise-longue. Nigel had a beer. The room seemed right; if he noticed such things he must be getting better. Nigel was gently pressing him. Oh well.

'Once upon a time there was a sixteen-year-old boy who was on a school trip to Spain.'

A quick little glance from Nigel.

'You, you mean.'

'Look, I said "Once upon a time" . . . this is literature, not autobiography. This poor seven-stone weakling, he was getting a bit brassed off with having sand kicked in his teeth the whole time by the guys who walked off with the girls while he read E. M. Forster. Anyway, suddenly on an impulse, he nipped off, cut away from the masters and school-fellows; he lost them deliberately, excitingly, in the back-streets of Barcelona (there's a title for you). He drank a cognac or two, then another. He wandered along the streets, heat coming up through his moccasins, until he saw a sign "British and Americans Welcome Here". How nice, he thought, the woman in the hotel may be a bitch but what extremely friendly people these Spaniards are.'

'You fell for it?'

Nigel was a good audience but he knew too much.

'He was a young sixteen, remember. Anyway, where was I?'

'Halfway down the slope.'

'Yes, well, he went in and sat down and called for a drink. He lit a long cool cigarette. You're never alone with a Strand; remember? No? Anyway, he knew a couple of words of Spanish and that was enough. The place was full of Americans, the Sixth Fleet was in town, all guns firing. A girl brought his drink and slid on to his knee. It was, you may say, satisfactory. In a very detached way she started man-handling him.'

'Really? God.'

Nigel, sitting on the floor, gulping his beer, was an excellent audience.

'Exactly. He was a bit of a flurry. Fortunately there was an American at the next table. He was as lucky as the boy was, he had a girl on his knee too. He thought he'd have a chat with him, so he took a deep lungful of smoke for extra poise and asked the American if he was married.'

'Oh God, *no*.'

'Look, boys grew up a lot slower in those days.'

'What did the American say?'

'He said,' James deepened his voice, '"You got nose trouble son?"'

'And you said?'

'The boy said, "I'm fine, thanks, but it is hurting a bit, it's been hot hasn't it, and rather stupidly I forgot to bring the cream I bought at the chemists."'

Nigel rolled around on the carpet, slapping himself.

'What's wrong? You see, he knew his nose was a bit red and thought this might be putting the American off.'

'It didn't seem to worry the girl.'

'Well that was the odd part. The cognac began to clear from his brain, he looked round, everyone had a girl, he was lucky as everyone else.'

'So what did you do?'

'He ran away. As fast as he could.' James stood up. 'Look let's go for a walk. I'm feeling much better now.'

Nigel suddenly went into the hall. He came back shyly and handed James a rolled-up poster.

'Is this for me? How very nice of you.'

James opened it. It was a large portrait of Virginia Woolf.

'Isn't she beautiful?' Nigel said.

'Yes, yes she is. *Very*. Thank you so much. I'll put it up. Where should it go?'

Nigel looked very pleased. He started to put his coat on.

'I'll leave that to you. I thought you'd like it. Mr Newman likes Virginia Woolf.'

'Does he? I didn't know that.'

'Yes, God, and did he get angry!'

'Really? Why?'

'Well, he was telling us about her novels, what she

believed in, and reading bits out. Have you read her? I'd never seen English like that before, let alone heard it, and then he went on to her group, and her death, the suicide and everything. He was very upset. We could tell.'

James listened, and nodded.

'Well, then he saw Miles Hopkins, who must have been grinning or something, and he said, "And what the hell" – only he didn't say that – "are you grinning about, Hopkins?!" And Hopkins said "If I wrote like that I'd kill myself too!"'

'What did Mr Newman do?'

'He walked over, grabbed him by the jacket and shoulders, threw him against the wall, then grabbed him again and kicked him, really kicked him out of the room, and slammed the door. It was, well . . . epic.'

'It was.'

James ran into the bedroom, pulled a couple of sweaters over his head, and joined Nigel in the hall. He could hear a garage door banging away in the wind, but he felt like a change, should he go and see her, why not. Someday he must tell Nigel about her, for the torn letters and the burnt photograph, by way of apologizing for his efficient understanding when Nigel revealed it. Could he explain that somewhere – perhaps between the conscious picture he had framed and the need he felt in his dreams – there was a person he wanted? But he must beware of those half-confidences, invented to ease the teller and disarm the inquisitive.

It was windy, his body felt cold, he felt little strength to resist it, but he stepped out. He wobbled a bit.

'Where do you live, Nigel?'

'Nearly half a mile or so, down River Walk, turn right at the supermarket.'

'I'll come as far as that.'

It was good to be about, a little warmth in him now;

they passed a few railwaymen. He liked deserted streets.

'Well, good-night, sir, see you in class next week.'

'Good-night, Nigel. No more "sir", all right? Thanks for coming round again. Next time I'll tell you about "The Student in the Bottling Factory".'

'I can't wait. Good-night.'

'And thanks for the Virginia Woolf.'

After ten yards or so Nigel glanced back and waved. That boy knew how to talk, he sensed the shadows behind words. James stood at the junction by the super-market and then, for no particular reason his jig-saw mind could place, he crossed the road and went down another street, past some small terraced houses. Thin wisps of smoke filtered up. A street of small back gardens, bicycle sheds, the kind of street which ended in a small parade of shops. Although he couldn't see the details now, the black and brown paint would be peeling off the outside windows, the curtains would be grey-white lace; they were the houses which endured, which, for no con-structive reason, made James feel guilty. He turned left into another street. The houses were bigger now, three storeys. Wall Lane. Tom's street. How odd he'd never been before, not even in his imagination; 'not much of a place', Tom said. They talked in the pub, the corridors, the classroom. It would be nice to see him, to have a chat. He'd missed him a lot.

Leaving the railway line on his left he went up the lane, tired but happy, 8 . . . 14 . . . 20 . . . 22. The last few were grey, faceless houses, obviously now flat-land. Three cardboard strips were stuck with rusty drawing pins.

22a P Scott
22b D T Woodbridge
22c T Newman The Man Who Beat Up Hopkins.

James pushed in the staircase light, a timed button, and climbed to the first floor where he paused for breath. His head ached. A scotch and cup of coffee would be just the job. Another ten steps and he was there. He rang the bell and stamped his feet, trying an exhausted Anapurna South Face expression, stamping, exhaling, keeping it going, Come on, Big Fella, I want to shake that Craggy Hand. Tom enjoyed melodrama.

Silence. Perhaps he wasn't in. The staircase light snapped off. There was a light in the flat. James rang again, started to go downstairs, then heard a door open deep inside the flat, 'Yeah, coming.'

Tom peered out, doing up his collar. 'Who is it?'

James pushed the staircase light on again. 'Hullo, Tom, it's me, sorry to barge in so late. I just felt a bit better, went for a stroll and thought I'd look you up. Sorry, it looks as if you'd gone to bed.'

'No, I hadn't gone to bed,' he said strangely, 'but I'm a bit tied up at the moment.'

It was tactless to call. As he turned to go, muttering, 'See you around', he looked past Tom into the hall.

'Yeah, good-night, see you James.'

Before the door closed James saw an overcoat and scarf lying over a chair. Helen's.

Chapter Twenty

He stumbled down into the street and ran and ran. He ran, sweating and panting hard. How long, how long, turn right, how long, has this, been going on, oh Christ. He stopped to get his breath. A man walked by, looking at James. He ran on, his mind pulsing with blood. Tom and Helen. In bed, of course they were in bed. On her, Tom. On ya Tom. On you Helen. Lie on her. The muscles in his arm, the stitches in hers, his smile, her back, broad back, her long legs, throbbing, urgent, the one with the knockers, pressing. He dragged his feet to the flat, got in and lay on the carpet. He didn't put a light on, he didn't want a light on. He smelt himself, his vest and shirt, the damp sweaters, his ears pumped. He coughed, the dust made him cough.

He'd seen less of them! Of course he'd seen less of them. Tom had been busy, pre-occupied since half term. Occupied. All right, OK OK, fine, if that's the way it is, that's the way it is, let it slide, let it go. When I want them and it's hard to know how, I can't, and if you don't want them you just do it. You just do it. What the hell if Jenny is pregnant, so bloody what, why make an issue of it, there's no mystery, you just do it. When the door bell goes you have to stop, there'll be another chance, you slip out and answer the door. You just do it.

James lay there, his mind running loose, his damp body

slowing down. He couldn't go back to school, that was definite. Yes he could. He must.

Tom and Helen, side by side. Tom was laughing at her, you like it with the light on, do you, good for you, OK by me. Helen was laughing quietly. Tom laughed. She enjoyed his firm hand running down the nape of her neck, she liked that, that was good, mm, that's good, you like it uh? I've got all of you, she said, she stared, wildly into his eyes, that's right Tom, it was oh it was good, good, it was beyond everything, her eyes stared, oh my God, her legs shook, she threw back her shoulders, she wanted this big Australian, she wanted, all of him, she was screaming, Tom was a scream, everyone said so. Tom was a real scream.

James stood up. He turned on some lights. He looked at his watch. Ten-thirty. He felt empty and clear-headed. He sat at his desk. He thought. He knew what to do. He shivered. Yes. That was right. He went to the bookshelves, where was that one, in an anthology. It had the right feel. Larkin. He pulled it out, found the right page and read it. Yes. He turned on the angle-poise, picked up his pen and wrote, shaking a little, but very neatly. 'For Tom Newman' on one piece of paper, and then he wrote on another piece, in exactly the same way, 'For Helen Craven'. He took out two envelopes and addressed them carefully and put a stamp on each.

He then read the poem again, and wrote on the first sheet

Love
The difficult part of love
Is being selfish enough,
Is having the blind persistence
To upset someone's existence
Just for your own sake –
What cheek it must take.

He paused. His heart was hammering again. He picked up the second sheet and copied out the same lines, so that it looked identical. He compared the two sheets. Now, the second verse on both pieces of paper, not shaking now, a little calmer.

> And then the unselfish side –
> Who can be satisfied
> Putting someone else first
> So that you come off worst?
> My life is for me.
> As well deny gravity.

Why waste hundreds of words? I don't want to *talk about it*. When he saw them again he'd look the other way: he didn't want to talk about it. At the Tuesday Common Room meetings they always sat together. Well, they wouldn't. Face that when it comes. Distaste rising in his throat, James wrote the third verse. His stomach clutched him.

> Yet, vicious or virtuous,
> Love still suits most of us;
> Only the bleeder who
> Can't manage either view
> Is ever wholly rebuffed –
> And he can get stuffed.

Let them choke on it. Let me choke on it. Was I good, Tom? Very. Was I? Very. He sealed the envelope to Helen. At the bottom of Tom's he suddenly scribbled, 'What business is it of mine, anyway? Why shouldn't you screw each other?' He then sealed it.

Back in the kitchen James drank some water at the sink. The coldness soothed him. He refilled the glass and went back to the sitting-room. Taking a few deep breaths he picked up the phone, dialled and waited. It rang and rang. Oh why didn't she, why in God's name didn't she get a phone by her bed? His head started to drum.

'Hullo, who is it?'

'It's me, mother, James, sorry it's so late. I must have woken you up.'

'What's wrong, what time is it, is anything wrong, dear; it's very late isn't it?'

'Yes, well, it's eleven-thirty, mother; I'm sorry. There's nothing wrong, I just wondered if I could come down for the weekend?'

'But of course, dear, how nice. What a surprise! Yes, do.'

'Good, well I'll be there about one o'clock to half past. Don't wait up.'

'One o'clock – you mean for lunch, dear? How do you mean, do you mean you're coming down now? Perhaps I'm not concentrating.'

'Yes, mother, I'd like to come down tonight. Please don't wait up. I've had a bit of a virus and I'd like to go straight to bed.'

'Of course I'll wait up, dear. I'll get you a little supper, you sound a little flat, don't you think you . . .'

'Look, *don't wait up*,' he shouted. 'I mean it, *go to bed*! I'll see you tomorrow morning. Thanks, mother, thanks, but don't.'

'All right, of course, whatever you say.'

'Good-night then, see you tomorrow morning.'

James sat, staring at the phone, drinking the water. Better get away, after you've written a note to Ian. He did that, then gathered together a few things: shaver, pyjamas, some books, toothbrush, pulled up the sheets and turned off the lights. His fingers fumbled the garage lock; he put his case on the back seat and placed the two letters and note beside him. He backed out. There was one light on in Ian's. Leaving the engine running in the road he tip-toed up the drive and dropped the note through the letter box. He should have rung but he didn't want to hear any caring enquiries from Liz or to make any slick explanations himself. He'd take this in his own way and deal with Tom and Helen in his own way. When he got out of town he'd post the letters, they would arrive on . . . hell, it was Friday night. They wouldn't arrive till Monday. That was too late, too damned late. Drive round to their places, what better than now, when they are still hot. He U-turned, drove past the College and through the town. The supermarket stood there, glaring and dull, waiting to be opened. An hour or so ago he was here with Nigel, only an hour or so ago, along these streets, feeling life returning. Describing and analysing houses to himself. He drove quietly, slowly, up Wall Lane and stopped a few yards short of 22. No lights. Was she still there? Were they talking, regretfully, in the dark? Deliver both letters there, yes, that would really hurt. Well, she's living with you, isn't she? We're all liberal, aren't we?

James opened the car door and stood still for a few moments, the letters awkward in his hand. Then he quickly dropped Tom's in the letter box. Hers too? Or was she lying in her bed, cold, waiting for morning? He turned back to the car, crumpled her letter in his hand, and drove off. A mile or so out of town, where the last houses dropped away, he stopped at a lay-by on an exposed stretch. He tore the letter up into little pieces and threw it all into the big wayside bin.

By day it was a pleasant enough drive, although the nurtured quiet wealth of the south east irritated him; he usually muttered 'money-bags', like Alan Priestley, as he drove through the cloudless roundness, past the over-dressed lawns and expensive little shops, house names nailed to trees, turn left for the stables, and do mind the horses. But you're part of it. By night he could see none of it and was glad. He did not have to react. Drabness suited him; he wanted it. His body and mind felt untuned, slack.

The car moved towards Wickleford, turning left or right as required. Some light rain began to fall. Twelve-fifteen, only another twenty miles. He put on the wipers. Slowly, the country, even in the dark, became familiar. That was Myrtleford. What would Tom think of the letter? Who cares? Let the bastard read it, swallow it. He gripped the steering wheel.

He was home. He pulled on the hand brake, locked the car and looked up at the house. The outside light was on, she'd be waiting in her room, and when the door shut she'd turn over and go to sleep, now that he was in. James walked round the side of the house. He could smell dead nettles and weeds. They needed some help down here. Tomorrow he must make an effort, he must talk.

The hall smelt, as it always did, of apples and polish, of years of care. He slipped past the tables, up the stairs, and across the first-floor landing. He put on the next landing light. The little tables, the worn carpet. Go to bed, don't think, don't feel any more.

He pushed open his door. He could smell the bookcase, the curtains. He looked at the bed, the sheets were starched and a hot-water bottle lump lay halfway down. The smell of lavender on the bed. He washed, looked at the old bookcase as he dried – all the old favourites were there – and settled into the white sheets, rubbing his feet on the hot-water bottle. He took out his contacts and put the light off.

Whenever he closed his eyes they throbbed with tired-ness, the swollen veins niggled at his lids. He gave up and turned on the light. He got a book from his case. How many times he'd walked this road: 'Anne recollected with pleasure . . .' Soon he was steadied by the balanced sentences, and when he paused to look up, he did not see Helen and Tom, but Anne Elliot and Bath; and then lifted away by *Persuasion*, he saw only the ceiling, until – with the light still on and the novel resting on his chest – he found sleep.

Chapter Twenty-one

The curtains were pulled back.

'Thanks, mother, thanks. How are you? You look fine.' She put down his cup of tea and sat down composedly on the bed. She looked older.

'That's very kind of you, James. But you, I'm afraid, look very tired. You left your light on. You've been ill . . . I can see that.'

'I'm over it now. Too much reading late at night!' Tom would have read the letter by now.

'If you came to see us more often, I could look after you properly. What would you like for breakfast?'

'Anything, really.'

'You always say that.'

She, no doubt, had been up hours, hoovering, peeling potatoes, getting Uncle David ready, doing her hair, making up, making sure the details were right. Her trivial round, scrupulous and thorough. Mother must have been very beautiful. She still was.

'What's the time?'

'Just after nine, it's a bit dreary outside but I've got a lovely fire going and your favourite for lunch.'

Thank God he wasn't at the flat; thank God he was away from all that.

'Beef? Lovely. Fattening me up again, I'll go along with it.'

She looked a bit offended.

'That bookcase needs a dust. I didn't have time, I'm afraid. Well, I'll do some toast and tea for you, dear. You don't want anything more?'

'No, that sounds lovely.'

From his bed James could see, as he saw when a child, the clouds pushing past the tops of the pines. He told himself to get up, to put some life, however artificial, into things. Uncle David would be about. He put himself through a coldish shower and ran back to his room and turned up the gas fire. What would she be thinking now, in her flat, making her breakfast? Who would she be thinking of?

James looked up at the perfect italic lettering. His uncle, full of respect for the fourteen-year-old, wrote it out one holiday. 'A classic remains a classic only because a few hundred up and down England enjoy it so heartily that their pleasure becomes religious.'

'You'll know what that means,' his uncle said.

'Yes. Who said it?'

'Arnold Bennett.'

James dressed. Funny to be home again, the light switches where you expect them, the nice nobbles in the wooden floor, the sixth stair runner will still be loose, you can bet. Nine forty-five, what a time to go down. It was loose.

He looked at the sparse good furniture, the two small desks, the understatement of England. In the kitchen he opened the paper on the table and slowly turned the pages as he ate his toast. He felt his body go weak. It wasn't going to be easy to be chatty, the spurious energy brought on by the shower had gone, the small satisfaction of sleep had left him. Then he heard the step he wanted to hear; very slow. He pushed back his chair and waited. The door was half opened. Uncle David stood there, stooping on his stick, the left foot in a built-up shoe. He was wearing his old battered green jacket.

'Hullo, uncle, how are you? Good to see you.'

'James, this is a nice surprise.'

He didn't move to shake hands, leaning forward with both on his stick.

'How are you keeping?'

'Much the same, much the same, as they say.' He raised a hand to ward off the clichés, laughing, still quite brown from summer, still with his trousers rubbed shiny, a little bit older.

'Clichés, James, are on the increase. That Kingsley Amis spots them. But look don't let me interrupt your breakfast, I'll find somewhere to perch.'

James sat down and drank some tea. As his uncle passed slowly behind James said, 'Thanks for your letter, the last one. I didn't have time to answer so I thought I'd come down instead.'

'A much better idea. When you've finished, there's something I want to show you in the stables.'

'Oh, won't be a second.'

'Are you very busy at school, hard at it?'

'Pretty. Yes, it's been a hard term.'

Uncle. He'd never done a day's work in his life. Well, he'd done one, as a fifteen-year-old railway clerk, but in the middle of the afternoon he bumped into the desk and bled so much he never went back; much later, when James was eight or nine, uncle cut his arm falling down the cellar steps and they changed his blood, bottles and bottles of other men's blood, which kept on coming out, until something started to hold. Then one day while James was in Oxford, uncle made a mistake when shaving, but mother got to him just in time, more and more bottles. Just in time was too soon and uncle wasn't pleased. He was fond of quoting Epictetus, about 'receiving powers to the limits of which you will bear what falls, have you not received endurance?' and so on, but Epictetus was not enough that morning when he was shaving.

Now he was on words again.

'But the point is, James, they don't know what the words mean, they don't use dictionaries, don't even know what the *OED* is. I can tell. They drop words like evacuating birds – and if we can't use words precisely what is the . . .'

James listened and prompted. What would he say when he next saw Helen?

Mother came in from the garden, smiling at the scene. She tapped James on the shoulder as she bent over. 'At it already, are you? Just let me clear away.'

'Look, I'll do it. Let me, you have a rest.'

'Don't be silly, I don't want a rest. Go on talking, you two.'

She started to fold the tablecloth, stroking it into shape. James stood up.

'I'd just like to have a look round, see how the old place is. I won't be long.'

He turned at the door and looked at his mother and uncle, 'It's nice to be home.'

He loped, two by two, up the stairs, beyond the bedrooms to the attic. Here, young and intense, he used to come on wet afternoons, his soul small as he looked out across the valley which fell away from the house. So he would read *Children of the New Forest* and a few years later *Silas Marner*. He forced open the swollen door, kicking the bottom, and crouched his way in. There was no electric light. The air was fusty and heavy. He looked round, cardboard boxes full of school exercise books. The broken window latch. The crunch of the rotting creosote floor. The smell of balsa wood painted with sickly sweet solution, a broken wing of an aeroplane. Here he watched the birds hanging in the air outside, wondering where they went. Here he had never been disturbed.

In the dusty silence James sat on the old apple box, his hands loosely together. Outside the blustery drizzle. Inside he could see little bits of fungus on the floor. He wanted to lie down, insensible, on that dirty brown mattress. But he couldn't.

Should he write to her? He'd try tonight. Was anything sayable? Would they be at it again today? He sat for half an hour, empty and shaken. Then he forced his mind aside, forced his feelings to skim on the surface, stood up and crouched his way out. He came down the stairs, across the landings, past the lavatory, down again to the hall, and outside, past the low hedge to the 'stables'. It was raining doggedly now.

James brightened his face as he went in. He couldn't see his uncle. Was everything else the same? Still there, the big blunt axe which he longed to use as a boy; still the old sacks hanging from the nails; dirty panes of glass, the rusty tap in the corner; birds got caught in the rafters, and he left his school trunk here, and once he found a sparrow with its head off.

Uncle David came across from his bench in the dark corner, his brown shiny face grinning; he pointed with his stick. He seemed more crumpled than ever, as the stronger leg pushed the made-up shoe ahead.

'Well, what do you think of it?'

'What?'

He waved at a new chrome and black invalid car, a polished chair with a little engine.

'A new one! When did you get it?' James hurried across.

'Last week, marvellous isn't it? Better batteries, easy to control and much nippier. I'm not so worried now about being hit from behind. Did twenty miles yesterday. Do you remember those lanes when you were young?'

Along those hedgerows, only black lines in his head-lights last night, he'd walked, careful to avoid any cars, pushing Uncle David, proudly identifying flowers to him; standing on the gates trying to see the moorhens in the ponds while uncle made up stories or pointed out how cows sat down. Over those fields he'd run, hell for leather, back for lunch.

'There are over five thousand different kinds of flowers and plants in England.'

'Really?'

'But you'll be lucky to find more than four hundred round Wickleford.'

And, half pulling the wheels himself, half pushed by James, uncle pointed out the easy ones, cow-parsley, ragwort, forget-me-nots, wood anemones, but do you know a Sweet Cicely, a Red Campion or Mugwort?

'Mugwort-mug-wort, what a funny name,' James half-ran, shouting, not too fast, skipping behind the chair.

Tilting his curved back towards the new machine, Uncle David pointed out the features, the positions of the cushions, while James approved.

'And look at the tyres. They'll last all right. Now what I intend is getting out in Bodiham woods, taking a few sandwiches and a rug, and read for an hour or so. It's high time I gave your mother a good break from me, she's looking after me morning and night. And the whole job is free; they've got consciences about us now, they used to leave us alone, like wounded animals. Funny old world, isn't it?'

'Yes, it is.'

'The open air, that's my niche, the Wordsworthian remark on your card. I loved that. You know if things had been different I might have made a decent farmer or gardener. When I was young I remember being scratched by corn and thinking that it was a good feeling, even though it put me to bed – I don't know, perhaps I idealize. I'm out of touch.'

'I don't think your are. And I think you new machine is great.'

'Would you like to try it!'

They laughed.

'How are you, James? I mean really? I'd like to know.'

'Oh fine thanks, a bit of a bug, but I don't want Mother to fuss.'

'I see, ah well. And later on tonight tell me what you're reading. I don't want to bombard you now. Come and see me after dinner, would you, I want to say something to you? But go and see your mother now, she's so excited you're here.'

'All right.'

But he didn't. James went to his room and lay, unpleasant, on his bed. Soon he was asleep, until at one o'clock his mother, kind and meticulous, called him for lunch.

For the rest of the day James tried hard and, for the most part, successfully. For an hour or more he kept up on how lovely Wales was, even pretended he had plans for his career. He was bland and he pleased. After tea he read until seven when he sat with them both, stoking up the fire, drinking large sherries. He chatted his way warmly through the meal, allowing his eyes to wander over the ornaments on the dresser, all in their right places. Then he was the man: he helped with the plates, he put on some logs (it was nice to have him down for a couple of days). Uncle David left them alone for a while. So much needed doing outside, mother said, she'd like his advice tomorrow. No bother, honestly, he said.

Gradually she lost concentration and fell asleep in her favourite chair, her mouth slightly open, slightly un-dignified. She'd been on the go all day and there was little more she could do, wasn't it lovely of him to come down; just when you'd thought he'd completely forgotten you, he turned up half-ill like this.

James turned on the T V. He slipped his shoes off and, in a desultory way, watched some zany American sculptor walking round London with a wheel rim in one hand and a piece of chalk in the other (and a camera crew somewhere). It was all a bit irritating. When he came across a building or angle that took his fancy he propped the wheel against it, stood back, had a good look and then – if 'moved' by it – drew a chalk line around the shadow in the sun which fell from the rim on to the pavement or step or whatever it was. Fairly silly. Oh, I don't know, there were some beautiful shapes left. Then he found himself in a grubby alley, or in front of large shabby buildings or the imposing façade of a gallery. He had an idea. He tried it out. Then, a week or so later, the sculptor returned to see what the wind, dust and rain had done. Sometimes his mark was still there, his angle, sometimes it had gone. Either way he did more drawings. He walked on up the busy street with his wheel and chalk. Credits.

'What do you make of that?' He hadn't heard his uncle come back.

'I'm not sure. Quite interesting.'

'Emperor's clothes, nothing more.'

'I'm not so sure,' James said, turning the T V off. 'We "cannot cage the minute" and all that. I suppose he felt he'd found some kind of intelligible pattern – for a moment. A strand, a touch of something that held it together, you know, him, chalk, the city, the elements.'

Uncle David smiled indulgently but pleasantly.

'You've been reading too much.'

'Maybe.'

'James, could we have a word now? Put some Schubert on, would you, don't want to wake your mother up, you know what I mean. I'll make my way off and see you in my room.'

'Shall I bring you a drink?'

'No, but bring yourself one.'

He could hear his uncle whistling as he went across the hall. One man went to mow, went to mow a meadow. The Schubert began. He stroked his mother's head as he went past.

'Here we are. Put the fire on, will you?' The dark mahogany sideboard, the bed and soft-sided chairs, the big old radio with the lovely circular dial. You could get anywhere in the world on that radio.

Instead of settling in his usual place, on his high stool, Uncle David moved to the side of his bed and groped around under a pile of papers. He took his time, unhurried by James, then came back with a large envelope, smiling, on his guard. Conveying the atmosphere of a special conversation he looked through the contents of the envelope. Suddenly he threw back his head with decision.

'I wonder if you'd look through these papers. I don't want to bother your mother with it. It's a little statement, really, I only want you, Dr Baines and a couple of others in the village to know. It's something I want you to think about, to bear in your mind.'

James read the form.

The purpose of this Declaration is to indicate to the doctor one's wishes in the event of there being no reasonable prospect of recovery from serious illness expected to cause serious distress or to render one incapable of rational existence. It does not ask the doctor . . .

Holding the paper firmly James looked into those interrogative, trusting eyes.

'I see, uncle. Shall I read it all now, or later?'

'Now, please, if you wouldn't mind.'

I request that I be allowed to die and not be kept alive by artificial means and that I receive what quantity of drugs may be required to keep me free from pain and distress even if the moment of death is hastened. This Declaration is signed and dated by me in the presence of . . .

The rest was blank, dotted lines.

'Now, you can't sign it, James, being a member of the family and you're going to benefit in my will, my share of the house and all the books, but I wanted you to know in case anything happens and there's any fooling around.'

'Is anything likely to happen?'

What about mother?

'I've had a couple of bad moments lately, it shouldn't be too long.'

When James spoke, he caught his breath, as if he was lying.

'And, you know, you're sure . . .'

'Yes, it's a marvellous feeling, not that I'm another Petronius Arbiter or Socrates, I wish I were, but I do want to move off when I want to. Seems eminently reasonable to me. When I saw you today I knew I could tell you. And getting the new car, that chair, is a great joy, it makes me leap out of bed. I can get away and around like a new man. I'll know what I'll be missing.'

But what will she have to live for?

'Will you tell mother?'

'No. You can tell her afterwards. She's very contented at the moment, it'll only make her miserable if I do. She'll be on the look out the whole time.'

Like last time. Was it wrong, an unworthy pressure to ask?

'But uncle, what will she do? You know she lives for you.' He laughed quickly as he put the forms back in the envelope and tucked it back where it came from.

'I've thought of that, of course I have. She also lives for you and she must also live for herself. Should I live for her?'

'I don't know, uncle.'

'People are very adaptable. I've noticed that. They always learn, people change, attitudes change. Thirty or forty years ago words that were dirty are now only soiled, and some clean ones of those days have got mucky. I've been meaning to write to you openly about all this but it doesn't go down too well on paper, too dramatic, now we're here and can talk about it as easily as this.'

'I'm very glad you've told me. Very glad.'

'Good. Now go and get yourself another whisky.'

                                              Saturday evening.

Dear Helen,

As I might not be seeing you again for a while I thought I'd write. I'm in my room at home (not my flat, my real home) and I've had an extraordinary day. I've felt every emotion in the last twenty-four hours. My friends, my mother, my uncle, seeing and hearing the most devastating things. You won't understand all that; it's by way of clearing the ground to say something to you.

I haven't seen you for over a week and we haven't spoken, except on the phone, since Wales. And now I'm trying not to think of you, and thinking of you.

James put down his pen. What was the point of all this?

When would Uncle David do it? He must have exactly

the right dose, the dose that didn't make you vomit – he'd read about this somewhere. He seemed so confident. You didn't have to risk the stomach pump. James's stomach turned. God, no, surely to God he wouldn't, he wasn't going to drive that new chair into a lorry, make it look like an accident, or deliberately be hit from behind wide out on a bend. Were all those forms just to say if there's anything left breathing on the road let me go?

He drove his mind back to Helen. He picked up his pen.

In fact I wrote something to you on Friday night but did not send it. Whether I'll send this or not I don't know. When you've just been told by your uncle he's going to kill himself you want to tell the truth: I understand why you wanted Tom. I can see it. I loathe the belonging, possessive notion with every fibre of myself, yet I feel it, and know its force. The feeling is inescapable. Some would call it love. 'Since there's no help'. . . . Anyway –

Candour or pretended candour, evasion or truth? James saw the words striving for a little dignity. He put the letter aside and lay on his bed.

He was writing the wrong letter. Suddenly he jumped up and grabbed another piece of paper.

Dear Uncle,
Thank you for telling me. I trust you and you can trust me. I hope you enjoy your new freedom. It's good to think of you seeing more of the countryside.
    Yours ever,
    James.

He went quietly downstairs. The hall was cold. He listened at his uncle's door. Breathing. He slipped inside, ran his hand along the mahogany sideboard and walked stealthily to his bed. He looked down, just seeing his face. He left the note on his bedside table.

'Must you go so soon, James dear?' she asked as he helped to wipe the dishes.

'I really must get back I'm afraid, but it's less than a month till I see you again.'

She held his hand, wanting him longer; it wouldn't be so bad if they'd really talked. Still, the two men had. There'd be something to remember. Why was she so silly: going to sleep after dinner. He looked so gloomy and irritable at times (no, no, tender and sad, like his father).

James put his things in the car and ran back inside. He looked younger in his polo neck sweater.

'Please don't come out, mother, it's still nasty, please don't. I've said good-bye to uncle and I'll ring you soon. Thanks for a lovely weekend.'

They hugged and parted; the quicker the better, they both felt. She smiled and waved as the Mini drove away, then walked back inside and upstairs to change the sheets so they would be ready for him next time.

By the time he got back, at four o'clock, the flush of the sitting-room fire and the claret had worn off. His mouth was dry; he could do with a cup of tea. Once more he climbed up the stairs, knowing he must get back into things, be really practical and mature – for Uncle David. In the half light he could see an envelope pinned to the door. 'James.' He opened the door, dropped his suitcase and read the note in the hall.

James,
Where the hell are you? I've been trying to find you all weekend. Please come to my flat when you get back. *Any time*. I've had my come-uppance.
    Tom.

He read it again, shoved it in his pocket and ran down the stairs.

Chapter Twenty-two

The door opened.

'James, hell, here you are, come on in.'

'Thanks.'

James walked past him so that Tom talked to his back.

'Where've you been, uh? I've been ringing you up, calling round, ringing you up –'

'I went to see my mother and uncle. I thought it was about time.'

'I didn't think of that.'

'You should have asked Ian.'

The sitting-room was a drab place. Three chairs and a poor-looking table. The television on spindly legs in the corner emphasized the emptiness. No wonder he'd rather live in the pub. There was a half-empty suitcase on the floor. If the bedroom was this grim, how awful for that too; but then the place didn't matter. You didn't need a cottage and an open fire.

'Sit down, throw anything in your way on the floor. Like a coffee? The kettle's just boiled.'

'Yes, I would.'

As Tom went past James glanced at him for the first time. He wasn't ugly or anything. On the floor, between the chairs, were small piles of shirts, socks and sweaters. James leant over and turned up the gas fire.

'Yeah, that's right, it's a lousy day,' Tom said, handing him his coffee.

He sat down opposite James. The overhead light was ugly. James hated it.

'Thanks for the coffee. The note you left. What's the problem?'

'Look, James, let's do the other first. It's a bloody mess and I'm sorry. There's no way in the world I can talk round it and don't want to.'

'I don't want to talk about it at all.'

'You're going to. I bumped into Helen a week or so before half term on the train down from London. Then the same thing a few days later, by chance. We had a nice chat, nothing in it. About you in fact. Then I met her in the supermarket a week ago, we walked back to her place. And then one thing and another. You know.'

'I know.'

Tom ran his hand over his mouth.

'Look, James, do you want to get on to fault, blame, all that, if you do, if that's the only way you get things, it wasn't Helen's fault it was mine.'

'I don't get things at all.'

'There was *nothing much* in it,' Tom said.

'Just sex.'

James didn't want his mouth to quiver.

'Yes.'

Stop quivering.

'While I was ill?'

'Yes.'

James looked round the room. Nothing to look at.

'I feel terrible about that,' Tom went on.

'I don't feel too pleased.'

'Let's leave it, James.'

'Fine, yes, let's leave it, that would be best, then it's all nice and unmessy. Yes, good, well we've cleaned that little one up. Now what about the note?'

'I had a telegram at eight on Saturday morning. Jen's lost the baby.'

'God, Tom, how awful. Hell, I'm sorry.'

'Yeah, nice and messy, but they cleaned that little one up too.'

'Hell, I'm really sorry, how terrible. Poor Jen. I'm so sorry.'

'Yeah, I am too.'

Tom was quiet. For quite a long time.

'Come on, let's go over to my place, I'll get you a meal.'

'Leave me alone, will you.'

James collected up the coffee cups and took them into the kitchen. He washed them up, then stood around. Tom came in heavily.

'Sorry. I've been with it all weekend. No one to talk to.'

'You should have gone to Ian or Liz or . . .'

'I didn't bloody want to go to bloody anyone, I wanted to tell you.'

Tom suddenly laughed at himself, nastily. 'Like a Hardy novel, isn't it? Except that I don't believe in Hardy's novels.'

'I do,' James said, 'I always have done. How's Jen? Is she all right, you know . . . in herself?'

'Na, she's not. She's in hospital. I rang up, they didn't say that in the telegram, but I thought she'd be bad. Severe depression – likely to be in for a while.'

Tom took two cans from the fridge and they went back in the main room.

'Isn't that normal – in these cases?'

Tom laughed, nastily, again.

'I knew she'd get me. I knew she wouldn't leave me alone over here. Normal? Yes, it sounds normal. I'd be depressed, wouldn't you?'

James looked round the room: the case, the clothes, which explained it.

'When are you going?'

'Tuesday, I've got a flight. The Head's been bloody good, like my dad would have been. Given me December's pay as well, and told me he can fix my timetable.'

'Well, it'll be exams in two weeks,' James said. 'When's the flight?'

'Three-thirty, Tuesday afternoon.'

'I'll take you to the airport.'

'There's no need. I've ordered a taxi.'

'Well, cancel it, I'm taking you. I'll see the Head and get the lunchtime staff meeting off.'

'The Head wants me to attend that,' Tom said.

'Well, I'll take you after lunch.'

A day passed and brought their parting closer. James wanted to be with Tom. Tom wanted to be alone. James moved dully around the school, ignoring everyone except Tom. All the poems and passages in class seemed horribly relevant or pointless and silly. James couldn't escape. His classes were glad to see him back.

'Thank you. Yes, I'm feeling fine now.'

'There's a rumour going round, sir, that Mr Newman is leaving, sir, is it true?'

'Yes, I'm afraid it is. Tomorrow. He's flying back.' The class protested.

'And is it true his wife's died?'

'No! Who said that? No, that's a silly rumour and please do all you can to stop it. She's ill in hospital, and he's going back to see her, as you'd expect.'

'He's a great bloke, sir.'

'Yes, he is.'

'Better than . . .'

'Thank you, there's no need to . . .'

Later in the morning Nigel came hurrying into James's classroom.

'But he hasn't even been here a term.'

'I know that, Nigel, as well as you do.'

'Oh hell,' Nigel said. 'Who'll we get instead?'

'I don't know. Probably a double dose of me.'

On their last night together James took Tom to the pub, and they put a brave face on it.

'Everything ready, then? Yes, two lagers, please.' Tom's eyes were a bit wild, nervous with worry, dreading the leavings, the arrivals and what he would find.

'More or less. I'll get it finished later. I can't stay too long. I've got some phone calls to make and a couple of people to visit.'

'Of course. And make sure you get a good night. Do you want some pills?'

'You'd give me too many, you bastard,' Tom laughed.

'Oh, come on!'

They didn't speak much. In the long silences they listened to the next table.

'How did your weekend go?' Tom said.

'Oh, very quietly, really.'

'I never did meet your mother and uncle; I'd like to have seen where you come from.'

Don't do anything, uncle, not yet; I must see you again.

On the next table there was a middle-aged couple, as ordinary and nice as the bar. She was drinking a half pint, he a pint. Their daughter, the clever one it seemed, was about to arrive unexpectedly for a few days from college and should they kill the fatted calf and buy a bottle of wine, ridiculous price though it was over the counter, or pop in for a few with her later?

'Whatever you think best, darling,' she said.

'No, I'll leave it to you, dear. And would you like the other half?'

'Yes, do you know, I think I will.'

Tom and James grinned.

'Do you want me to come back with you?' James asked. 'Anything I can do? Tidy up the mess you Australians always leave?'

'No, I'll be right, thanks. Pick me up after the staff meeting and I'll get the hell out of your life.'

Another woman came into the bar, looked round, and went across to the contented couple. The husband brought her a drink. She sat down very tidily as if up to no good. They all put their heads close while the woman talked quietly, urgently, to them. They all looked a little unhappy, sat back and shook their heads slowly.

'Ah, back in the land of the living,' Alan said.

'Yes.' James looked at the large brown envelope in his pigeon-hole. Inside he found a letter and a large photo.

Dear sir(s),

Why I call you 'sir' when you've asked me not to I don't know but I rationalize I would if I met you in a pub. Anyway who cares?

So, *sir*, please thank Mr Newman, I mean *really* thank him for his lessons on love poetry. (And you, of course, for yours. But you're still here, thank God, and what this dump would be like without you, God knows; but enough of this *outsplurge*.) The point is I've tried to find Mr Newman but can't: he isn't at his flat, and he doesn't take us till Wednesday, which is a bit late to thank him as he'll be over India or Singapore or somewhere. So will you please tell him his lessons have been an oasis. 'A bloody oasis', Paul Scott said.

I enclose a photo Paul Scott took of you both (and me!) with his long-range lens. Don't you look funny!

'Happy Christmas and Good-bye' to Mr Newman. Who knows, I might even make it to Australia one day?

Yours, Nigel.

James looked at the large photo. It was obviously taken at the Masters' Rugger Match. The camera brought Tom and James close together, foreshortening the distance between them. James was on the touch-line, looking very wet, with one hand raised in the air, explaining something to Nigel. In a balloon out of his mouth James was saying 'Read a Pinta Play A Day'. Tom was in the distance, on the pitch, covered in mud. Nigel had written in the balloon out of Tom's mouth 'Bash A Pom A Day'.

'12.45. SHORT MEETING. REPORTS', the Head's notice said; and 12.45 it was, not a minute later, when the Head walked in. The September suntan may have gone but the term was not over by a long chalk.

'Gentlemen, before we get on to reports, which Colin has asked we discuss today, I'd like to make a plea: this is always a long term, probably the hardest of the year, so let's tighten up over these last difficult weeks. The weather gets worse, the boys get worse, let's make sure we don't. We can already look back on this term with some satisfaction, so let's not be ragged in this vital Oxbridge and school exam period.

'Now I've had a note about reports. You know my position of old on this, but it may bear repeating. They should be written with fountain pens, not biro, especially not red biros which are for marking only, and they should be constructive and encouraging in tone. Err on the side of generosity. No one likes to be damned in print. Say harsh things, if you have to, face to face; don't write them. I think I'm only really talking about common-sense. I know sometimes "satisfactory" seems the only appropriate word, and indeed many of us would probably settle for that as a definition of ourselves, but let us try to write it at greater length.'

There was a pause. They all had common sense, they all agreed with the Head. But silences embarrassed Colin so he took rather longer to say the same thing and, as compassion was in the air, Alan spoke, and then Colin again, hoping the Head hadn't minded him bringing up this hardy annual. The Head drummed his fingers.

'Good, I think we're probably all agreed on this one. As I'm sure we are on the next. You may or may not know Tom Newman is returning to Australia because his wife is not well. This is obviously a most distressing business for him and he has particularly asked that he doesn't have to say anything today, and we of course understand that.

'Even in so short a time he's thrown himself into everything, and his vitality has been much appreciated by all who have come into contact with him. Only this morning, at the end of one of my massively dull Tacitus lessons, one boy told me, and boys are very good judges as I know to my cost, he was very sorry Mr Newman was going because his lessons were so interesting. How many of us make our lessons interesting?'

Not me, the room stirred and groaned.

'Tom Newman has touched all our lives with his sense of fun, his open nature and his energy. Despite his premature return we hope he will take back many happy memories of England, and we're happy to think he'll soon be reunited with his wife and helping her to a speedy recovery. Tom Newman, thank you.'

The Common Room applauded.

The Head had spoken well. After he'd left for his lunch the masters dispersed. Ian, Alan and his other friends moved towards a pale and shaken Tom to say their farewells. James slipped into the adjoining room to check if there was anything in his pigeon-hole. It was empty.

'Come round for a drink sometime,' Brian said, 'I haven't seen much of you this term.'

'Thanks, Brian, I'd like to. I'll give you a ring.' He waited for Tom to come through.

Chapter Twenty-three

The Mini, piled up with suitcases, laboured up the long hill.

'Do you think they'll let me on with that lot?'

'I should think so. Tell them the truth, you had to leave in a hurry.'

They drove on. Soon James filtered into the thick motorway traffic.

'Broken-windscreen country,' he said.

Tom's eyes moved across the landscape. 'It's all over so quickly, I can't believe England's come and gone.'

James half looked at Tom. He really was going.

'I hope Jenny gets better soon, she'll be so pleased to see you. She'll be looking forward to it all day.'

'And you get in touch with Helen, right? She'll want you to.'

James laughed doubtfully.

'She will,' Tom said.

'Maybe.'

Cars slammed by them, articulated lorries made the Mini rock a little. Was Uncle David out on the dangerous Canterbury road, driving at an exhilarating speed, precariously, about to press the brake?

Don't do anything yet, uncle. There's more to say.

James held firmly to the steering wheel. In the distance a big-bellied plane lifted itself into the grey. Tom looked nervously at his watch.

'We've plenty of time, don't worry. We're nearly there.'

'The end of the road,' Tom said with a small laugh, running his hand round his mouth.

'Oh, by the way, I've put an envelope into your green grip. It's got a letter in it, written to me actually, but about you, and a photo you might enjoy.'

Tom turned round to the back seat.

'I'll have a look at it now.'

'No, don't; later on the plane. It's not exactly Sexy Susan in a plain wrapper but it'll give you a good laugh.'

'I'll need one.'

The car turned off the motorway and along the cheerless approaches. As they entered the airport the road divided into three. 'Get in Lane. (1) Domestic Flights (2) Continental Flights (3) Inter-Continental Flights.' James looked in the rear-view mirror and moved into the appropriate lane.

'Why is Australia such a bloody long way?' he suddenly asked.

'I don't know, not my subject. Look, just drop me at the terminal. Don't hang around.'

'No, I'll park the car first and then I'll see you off, if you don't mind.'

Somewhere on the far side James found a place. He got out and handed Tom a case.

'Hey, James, it's been good – too bloody good.'

'Yes, yes it has.'

James put his head back into the car and slowly pulled out another case. His eyes ran round the car park for directions. Big signs told him where to go. Heavy with luggage, they walked together through the lines and across the damp spaces; their footsteps pressed open the parting doors and they went into the drab, glaring complex.